THE ALVAREZ GIRLS

J. E. ORTEGA

*For my sister who protected me at all cost and for all the military service member who never got to say **"me too."***

CONTENT WARNING

The Alvarez Girls:

This story contains depictions of violence, including physical assault, murder, and gun violence, which may be triggering to some readers. It also deals with themes of grief, loss, trauma, and emotional distress surrounding death, including the loss of a loved one. There are references to suicide, familial estrangement, and complicated family dynamics. The novel explores issues of systemic corruption and misogyny within institutional power structures. Please read with care.

PROLOGUE

"EL CAMIÓN DE LA BASURA!" Yaneriz yelled, tearing out of the house like a hurricane. She never thought about things like dirt or danger when there was fun to be had, and today was no different. Behind her, Amaya followed, still fumbling to keep up.

A week ago, it had rained nonstop in the Dominican Republic. Once it ceased, their uncles cemented their swing set and half of their backyard. But they ran out of money and didn't finish the rest. So the girls had a half-muddied, half-cemented backyard.

The excitement of the game overtook Yaneriz as she sprinted to the swing, never giving a second thought to the muddy ground or the broken glass that still littered parts of their yard. She wasn't one to consider consequences until it was too late, and today would be no different.

Amaya trailed Yaneriz and did the same, wanting to be just like her sister. But she didn't quite make it, at least not one of her chanclas. Amaya sighed as she tugged the sandal from the sticky mess and saw Yaneriz already at the swing, grinning in victory. Amaya loved her sister, but she didn't like always being a step behind.

With her chancla in one hand, Amaya ran to the swing. Once she reached the smooth cement, her muddy foot slid, and she put the chancla back on. Tight curls stuck to her temples. A bead of sweat hung on her upper lip. It smelled of rain and rust when the younger twin got to the swing.

Amaya hopped to the opposite side of the seesaw. But seeing the grin up close made her jaw tighten. She was born fifteen minutes after Yaneriz, and her twin constantly reminded her of that. Yaneriz was also faster than her, but never cared to use it unless it was to show off. Playing 'El Camión de la Basura' meant Amaya had to move as fast as Yaneriz to pick up all the imaginary trash from the imaginary street. Amaya loved and hated the game.

After thirty minutes of playing, Yaneriz yelled, "You are not picking up the bags fast enough!" The strong breeze whipped her face.

Amaya looked at the disapproving look on Yaneriz.

"I am," Amaya replied.

The curls on her temple had shrunk even more with the humidity. Her high bun was now bouncing on her nape, and Amaya's stomach burned with her sister's criticism. After a few minutes of letting Yaneriz think she didn't care, Amaya finally sped up.

"There you go," she heard her sister say.

Amaya's chest inflated with pride. A sentiment she didn't want to show Yaneriz. With the force of her swing, the breeze became spirited and cooled her scalp. This wasn't so bad, Amaya thought.

"OK, we finished our route. Now you gotto jump," Yaneriz said out of nowhere.

Amaya pictured the garbage man swinging with barely one foot and one hand on the truck. She wondered what it would feel like to fly and feel the air underneath her feet.

"Come on! You are being slow again."

Amaya gritted her teeth. She bent her knees and pushed

herself back. As far back as she ever could. When she reached the highest point, Amaya pushed her chest forward and jumped.

————

Yaneriz looked at the unfinished part of their yard, her sister's feet, and then noticed the charred glass. Why hadn't I seen that? Why didn't I make Amaya put her shoes on? She prayed what she imagined in her head would not happen. But everything moved so slowly and fast all at once.

Abuela told her to keep their shoes on. She had told Yaneriz she was in charge, and no, it wasn't fair. So anger rose in Yaneriz's belly at the unfairness of being born fifteen minutes before her sister. But it was something she couldn't fight, so she swallowed her pride.

Yaneriz tasted the humidity on her lips when she opened her mouth to say stop, but no words came out. Everything happened so fast, and before she could unclench her fists, she heard a shrill that dug into her bones and made her heart stop. Right then, all the anger bubbling in her stomach vanished.

————

The heat from the kitchen made La Doña's—Abuela's — loose gray hair stick to her face. She was cooking dinner. Today, Carlo's Nueva Yol money didn't make it, so instead of chicken, it was fried eggs with rice and beans. After the girls' mother ran off and married a gringo, Carlos followed. La Doña always thought raising children alone intimidated her son, which was why he still hadn't sent for them five years later.

She didn't mind taking care of her son's girls. In her early years, La Doña yearned for daughters. But age brought a weariness to her body that was hard to overcome.

She should have known Yaneriz screaming at the top of her lungs and running out of the house like a cyclone was not a good idea. Yaneriz had a lot of energy and pushed her sister to match it, which was why, when they were together, her sons called them El Cyclón. Still, La Doña didn't mind it. They should exercise their energy only safely. But someone hollering told La Doña safety had gone out the window, and she knew just who the instigator and hurt one were.

La Doña appeared at the door, her body heavy with age but her voice sharp. "Yaneriz!" she barked, though her eyes were on Amaya, bleeding and tear-streaked.

"What did I tell you about keeping your sister safe?" Her words hit like the blows from a chancla.

———

The oldest twin heard her grandmother, and she knew she had gone too far this time. Yaneriz watched Abuela lean down to check on Amaya. She watched as her grandmother's eyes found her again. She watched her grandmother's hand reach for her foot, and she knew the sting she had felt from her words would not be the only thing that would hurt her that day.

Yaneriz brought her hands to cover her face. At once, the chancla ricocheted off her back, legs, thighs, and shoulders. It hadn't stopped raining. It was raining chanclas.

"I told you to take care of your sister," Abuela said repeatedly with chancla blows.

Yaneriz's skin burned with every slap of the slinky rubber. But her words stung more because they seared through her flesh.

"Mamá," Amaya cried out from where she landed and finally made Abuela stop.

Yaneriz lowered her arms slowly and watched her grandmother walk back to her sister.

———

Pain seared through Amaya's leg. She looked at her right shin. Pink meat and half a piece of glass stuck out from the split skin. Blood oozed down her leg, between her muddied toes, and onto the dirt.

"Mamá," she cried again, her voice small and trembling.

Abuela crouched down, cradling Amaya in her arms. Amaya buried her face in the crook of Abuela's elbow, breathing in the scent that lived in her grandmother, Vicks, deodorant, and sazón.

"Respira, mi niña, respira," Abuela whispered, rocking her gently. Her voice was soothing, but when she looked at Yaneriz, her expression hardened. "¡Coño, Yaneriz! You're supposed to take care of your sister, not get her hurt!"

Amaya whimpered, tugging at her grandmother's sleeve. "Pero me duele, Abuela."

Abuela's voice softened as she stroked Amaya's head, but the anger still lingered. "Lo sé, mi amor, lo sé. We'll fix it." Then she turned back to Yaneriz, her tone sharpening again. "And you—mira lo que has hecho. Why do I have to keep telling you this? You're the oldest!"

Yaneriz flinched, wanting to say something, but she stayed muted. Her chest tightened with guilt.

Amaya's sobs broke through the tension. "Can't we fix it here? ¿Y Ramón?"

Abuela shook her head. "Ramón won't be back from la universidad for hours, and I'm not leaving you like this. Tenemos que ir al hospital ahora."

As they spoke, Yaneriz stood frozen, watching the blood trickle from her sister's leg. She opened her mouth to offer help. "Abuela, I—"

But Abuela cut her off with a wag of her finger. "No, tu te quedas aquí. Has hecho suficiente por hoy."

Yaneriz swallowed hard, her face flushed with shame. She nodded, knowing nothing she said would make it better.

Abuela sighed deeply, her anger slowly giving way to the weight of the situation. She rubbed her temples and took a deep breath before speaking again. "You can finish what I started so we can have something to eat when we come back. You can help your sister with that."

Yaneriz clenched her jaw. She despised cooking. But when she heard Abuela grunt while lifting Amaya into her arms, the weight of exhaustion in her every movement, Yaneriz realized that maybe cooking wasn't the worst thing. Without a word, she followed Abuela into the kitchen, her eyes glued to her grandmother's weary steps, knowing she needed to do something.

As she watched Abuela tend to Amaya, a strange pain shot through Yaneriz's leg. Her right shin throbbed, mirroring the injury she saw on her sister. She gasped, looking down at her leg, but it was unscathed. The pain wasn't hers. It was Amaya's.

Abuela's voice snapped her back to reality. "Esto va a detener la sangre, mi niña. Aguantate, ya casi casi te llevo al hospital."

Yaneriz looked at Abuela, her heart sinking with guilt. She could see the exhaustion on her grandmother's face. It wasn't just Amaya who was hurting—Abuela was tired, too. And it was because of her.

Abuela scooped Amaya into her arms again and headed toward the door. Before leaving, she turned to Yaneriz one last time. "You know where everything is, right?"

"Sí, Abuela," Yaneriz mumbled. She knew what that meant—the machete and revolver were always in the same place, just in case.

"Lock the door," Abuela added as she stepped outside.

"I'm sorry," Yaneriz whispered, her voice barely audible.

Abuela paused at the door. For a moment, it seemed like she hadn't heard. But then she turned, her stare cutting through Yaneriz like a blade. "Let this be a lesson. You're the oldest for a reason, Yaneriz. Not to push your sister around, pero para cuidarla. All you two have is each other. ¿Cuándo vas a entender eso?"

Yaneriz had never seen her grandmother so serious, so full of disappointment. The door closed with a heavy thud, and Yaneriz locked it as instructed. She stared out the window, watching as Abuela climbed onto the back of a motorcycle with Amaya on her lap.

Everything outside looked the same—the street, the houses, the sky everything moved alive—but for Yaneriz, the world had stopped.

And in that moment, she made a promise to herself: I will protect my sister.

CHAPTER
ONE

SEVENTEEN YEARS Later

As she stood at the top of the hill, a strange sensation crawled up her spine—an unsettling prickle, like a memory trying to surface. Her chest tightened, and for a moment, it felt as if something sharp had pierced her skin. Yaneriz froze, her breath catching in her throat.

The strange feeling gripped her, tugging at something deep inside, a memory she hadn't thought about in years. It felt familiar, like the day when she was a kid, and Amaya had cut her leg.

This was the same—an aching, phantom throb—only in a different place. Yaneriz placed her hand over her chest, feeling the pressure building, as though her heart wasn't entirely her own anymore. A pulse of anxiety spread through her veins, her skin tingling with the echo of a pain that wasn't hers but felt as real as the ground beneath her feet.

I'm okay. I'm okay, Yaneriz told herself. The camera she held shook as her grip weakened. She put it down and, feeling the weight of her client stare rotated her lens as if the focus was off. But it wasn't, at least not the camera's focus, but her own.

Her head bobbed in a slight nod, though her thoughts still whirled with doubt. She drew in a long breath, the air sharp and dry in her lungs, grounding her as she lifted the camera to her right eye. The familiar weight of the lens pressed against her hand, steadying the chaos in her mind. Focus. This is what she was good at, capturing the world through her lens. It had always been her escape.

Yaneriz tried to focus on Mari's photos, but her mind kept wandering back to Amaya. When was the last time they'd spoken? It felt like she'd been working non-stop, gig after gig, and suddenly it hit her—had almost an entire summer passed without a call from her sister?

She forced her focus back to the job until she noticed the gleam in Mari's face. She stopped and reached into her bag. "Here."

Her client, Mari, took the tissue from her and dabbed away the sweat. The sun in El Paso never let up. It beat down relentlessly, like it had something to prove.

"Thanks," Mari said after drying her face.

Yaneriz smiled as she tucked the tissues back into her bag. The strange feeling that had gripped her earlier had finally eased, and her heart had stopped its wild gallop. She was grateful for the calm, which allowed her to focus once again on Mari's graduation photoshoot.

She was a repeat client, and someone Yaneriz had come to know quite well through photography. This was Mari's second master's degree. Earlier, at the lookout point, she had bashfully admitted that she was considering a Ph.D. next. Knowing that Mari had crossed the border at just five years old and carried the weight of her family on her small shoulders ever since, Yaneriz couldn't help but place her in superhero status.

In fact, Mari reminded her of another superhero—

someone even closer to her heart. Someone who, growing up, had always tried to be as fast as her and as strong—Amaya.

For years, Amaya had tried to keep up, always chasing after her older sister even when Yaneriz didn't think it was a competition and eventually she did more than just catch up—she surpassed her. Yaneriz smiled at the thought, letting the deep sense of pride she felt for Amaya grow stronger.

"I think I got it," Yaneriz finally said when she snapped the best shot, capturing a thoughtful expression on Mari with the early morning traffic of Mexico and El Paso in the background. "It's pretty good."

She turned her camera around and let her client go through the pictures.

And while Amaya was fiercely independent, it sometimes worried Yaneriz. Her sister was so trusting, often in a rush to meet life goals that, in Yaneriz's eyes, didn't need rushing. Had all those childhood competitions given Amaya the wrong idea? Had Yaneriz inadvertently pushed her twin into thinking everything had to be a race?

Looking out over the city, Yaneriz felt the early summer breeze rustling her curls, bringing with it a wave of nostalgia. It reminded her of Abuela's gentle hand tousling her hair, a comforting, familiar touch.

The way Amaya had rushed into the Army never sat right with her. She had wanted to say something, but feared that pushing back would only drive Amaya further. It felt like a lose-lose situation and Yaneriz would never know if her silence had encouraged or slowed her sister's decision. Back then, Amaya had been too young, too trusting, and untested by the world. It had worried Yaneriz then, and in some ways, it still did.

Mari's voice cut through the silence, taking her out of her train of thought, but it sounded distant, like it wasn't meant for her. Yaneriz blinked, her brows furrowing as she glanced at her client. But Mari's expression seemed neutral. If anything, the longer Yaneriz looked at her the more uncomfortable Mari seemed to get.

"Did you call?" Yaneriz finally asked. She couldn't be sure, since it seemed like the breeze carried stray words like echoes.

Yaneriz watched Mari's face for any clue. A flicker of something—embarrassment?—passed through her client's face before she shook her head. "No."

"The wind is making me hear things," Yaneriz finally said sheepishly.

"It does get windy sometimes," Mari said, sounding just as uncomfortable as Yaneriz felt. She turned her gaze back to the camera, giving Yaneriz time to compose herself.

Mari scrolled through the photos, her lips twitching into a small smile. "These are really good," she said, nodding slowly. "I think they capture exactly what I wanted."

Yaneriz exhaled, relieved. "Glad to hear that."

"Give me a week," Yaneriz said, feeling her cheeks flush with embarrassment.

"Sounds good," Mari replied. She narrowed her eyes and Yaneriz could have sworn Mari wanted to say something, but the fleeting thought left her gaze and she turned towards the parking lot.

Yaneriz waited until Mari's car disappeared from view. Once it was out of sight, she dragged her hands down her face. "Goddess, I'm such an idiot."

She didn't believe God was a man and found it hard to accept that a being capable of birthing the world wouldn't carry a womb. It was something she and Amaya often disagreed on but had learned to avoid to keep the peace. Maybe she hadn't given her sister enough credit. After all, being mature enough to steer clear of certain subjects with someone you shared an amniotic sac with had to count for something. If Amaya could handle that, surely she could handle the Army and whatever came with it.

Yaneriz took a deep breath, calming herself. Mari wasn't judgmental, and she would likely forget this awkward moment by the time they meet again. And Amaya is fine, she reassured herself. I mean, I talked to her. But then, Yaneriz thought, When did I actually talk to her?

It was early morning on a weekday, and with some schools already on summer vacation, there was less traffic than usual. Yaneriz headed back to her loud green Beetle, which she affectionately called The Hulk, to check her phone. The days had blurred together.

She scrolled through her messages until she found Amaya's. A month. It had been a month. Yaneriz swallowed hard. That was far too long. Even when Amaya went to train, it was never more than three weeks. Never a month.

She pressed on her sister's contact with FaceTime, but there was no answer.

"Oye, llámame," Yaneriz said, recording a message for her sister.

She stared at her reflection. Her eyes filled with doubt, stared back at her. She licked her lips and tossed the phone into the car, only to hesitate and pick it up again.

'I'm going on a mini-vacay. Won't have reception. Call you when I get back.' had been her sister's last message.

Yaneriz had given it a thumbs up. She stared at the message again. A thumbs up. Why did I just give it a thumbs up? Looking at it now, felt as hollow as a coconut without the milk. A month? It wasn't like Amaya to disappear for that long, even on vacation. Yaneriz's stomach tightened with unease as she thought about that last text.

Her fingers hovered over the screen, itching to call again, but she hesitated. Even though this was rare, Amaya hated being badgered, and Yaneriz had promised to trust her. She said she would stop trying to mother her.

"Fifteen minutes, Yaneriz. You have never let me forget about those fifteen minutes," Amaya had said when Yaneriz had gone as far as driving to her place when she had been stationed in Fort Stewart. That time Amaya had gone three weeks without calling her back and Yaneriz thought the worst.

That hurt, but she had promised Abuela, and she had let her down before. She had let Amaya get hurt, fall on the glass and get hurt. She couldn't do that again. **All they had was each other**, that's what Abuela had said.

She looked out over the city, the quiet streets below a stark contrast to the growing noise in her head. The morning breeze that had seemed so familiar now felt unsettling, carrying with it the weight of unspoken words and a creeping sense of dread. It's probably nothing, she told herself, but the nagging feeling wouldn't let go.

With one last glance at her phone, she shoved it into her bag, trying to shake the discomfort settling in her chest. She turned the key in The Hulk's ignition, but as the engine sputtered to life, so did the thought she'd been trying to ignore:

What if something's wrong?

CHAPTER
TWO

YANERIZ SAT cross-legged on the worn couch in her El Paso apartment, her laptop balanced on her thighs as she clicked through the RAW images from that morning's shoot. The familiar glow of the screen reflected off her glasses, casting a soft light over the room. She leaned forward, adjusting the histogram on the first few shots, checking exposure, contrast, and color balance. Her finger hovered over the zoom function, enlarging each frame to inspect the sharpness and focus, ensuring she had captured Mari's expression just right.

This one's good, she thought, adding the image to the flagged folder.

She continued through the batch, adjusting levels where needed and marking the photos she'd cull for further processing. Yaneriz always trusted the technical side of photography. Numbers gave structure to the creativity. But as her eyes scanned through the thumbnails, she felt a heaviness settling in her chest, pulling her attention away from the screen. It was the same she had felt earlier when she was with Mari.

She sighed, rubbing her temples. *Focus, Yani.*

Her fingers grazed the trackpad, flipping through the images, each shot more technically sound than the last. But something felt off, something she couldn't quite name. She was trying to concentrate on the subtle details—the catchlight in Mari's eyes, the soft background blur, the perfect bokeh— but the sense of unease that had started earlier on the hill was only growing stronger.

Suddenly, she found herself staring at the screen without seeing anything at all. She blinked, pushing herself back from the laptop. The weight in her chest tightened, like a string being pulled, and she knew it wasn't about the photos anymore.

It was Amaya.

She glanced at her phone, which lay next to her, the last message from her sister still on the screen.

'I'm going on a mini-vacay. Won't have reception. Call you when I get back.'

Yaneriz swallowed hard, trying to shake the tension in her throat. Amaya had always been independent, but lately, she's been a bit more secretive than usual and Yaneriz respects her sister's privacy but thinking about it, Amaya had never kept things from Yaneriz.

Even if it was a two-day vacation, Amaya would have said more than that and the more Yaneriz thought about it, the more that she felt the string between them, the one that had always existed whether she acknowledged it or not, tugging harder. It was like when they were kids, when she could feel Amaya's cut as if it had been her who had it.

Her fingers hovered over the next image, but her mind was elsewhere, drifting back to their childhood. It had always been this way, hadn't it? Yaneriz was the oldest, the fast one, the protector, and Amaya, the one she needed to protect even when her twin didn't think so.

She leaned back into the couch, her breath shallow, her

intuition creeping up on her like a slow tide. The unease gnawed her. She stared at Amaya's last message again.

Yaneriz's brow furrowed. *Mini-vacay?* She scrolled up through their texts, her mind racing.

"Wait a minute." Yaneriz read through every text they had written to one another.

That was not Amaya. Mini-vacay was not in Amaya's vocabulary. Every text between them used Dominican short-cuts, an informal Spanish that, in long texts, turned into Spanglish. Their shared language served as a shorthand for expressing what they couldn't always articulate in English.

She scrolled until finding the text that didn't sound like Amaya.

'Yani! tú no vas a creer pero encontre un restaurante aqui que vende yaniqueque. Te arrecuerda cuando Abuela made Yaniqueque for us y yo empeze a llamarte Yaniqueque pero Abuela no le gusto eso.'

'I remember,' Yaneriz had replied

'y el Yani se te quedo,' her sister had replied.

'Unfortunately.'

'Don't act like that shit wasn't bomb.'

'What? The stupid nickname or the Yaniqueque?'

'Both ;-) '

'You can keep the nickname but send me a yaniqueque.'

'They are not like Abuelas. Not worth the postage.'

'okay, I'll let it go this time. Cuidate.'

'Yes, mom...'

She remembered that conversation. She remembered how the shame of being called mom by her sister stopped her from texting more. Amaya had gone to Kentucky for some work trip, and in Louisville, found a Dominican spot. She had been so excited when Yaneriz called her a few days after that text exchange. She said it was like returning home to the DR, and the two made plans to go back together. They hadn't gone in seven years. Not since both went back to bury their grandmother after Amaya had graduated boot camp. They knew it was too long and both had promised to plan a trip back this time under better circumstances.

Those texts were Amaya. That was her sister's voice—unmistakable. But as Yaneriz re-read the last message, the difference hit her like a wave. The shift in tone wasn't just strange; it was jarring, unsettling. The tension she'd been ignoring snapped into sharp focus. This wasn't just a gut feeling anymore. Something was unmistakably wrong.

Her pulse quickened. She had been brushing it off for too long, hoping Amaya was just caught up in work, but if Abuela were still alive, she would yell at her to get a hold of her sister and most likely throw a few chanclas her way.

She called her sister, feeling her stomach twist with each unanswered ring, and then the realization hit her like a gust of wind. She had to go to Killeen, Texas, where Amaya was stationed. Whether or not her sister called her mom, she had to make sure she was alright. Amaya might get mad, but that didn't matter. Yaneriz couldn't shake the certainty that Amaya needed her.

Her intuition—her twin sense—had been buzzing too long to ignore.

She grabbed her keys, slung her camera bag over her shoulder, and headed for the door. The photos could wait. Amaya couldn't.

Yaneriz locked the apartment, tossing her phone into the passenger seat of The Hulk. She set out to the airport to catch the first flight to Killeen.

I'm coming, Amaya.

WHO LIVES IN KILLEEN? Yaneriz thought as the plane landed at the small regional airport. The depressing vibes weighed heavily, pressing against her chest. Yes, it had way more greenery than El Paso, but something was off here—something unsettling. Too many bad things had happened in this place. She sighed, her breath fogging the plane's window.

As the plane rolled to a stop, she swung her camera bag over her shoulder. Amaya should've been stationed closer—at Fort Bliss. That thought only deepened her frustration. If Amaya had been closer, maybe none of this would be happening.

Yaneriz squeezed through the crowded aisle, dodging elbows and avoiding eye contact. She preferred to travel unnoticed, but as always, people were rude. Her brows furrowed when she caught a sharp comment in Spanish from a blonde woman with a sneer on her face. She didn't understand why people automatically assumed she didn't know Spanish.

Through clenched teeth, Yaneriz said, "Doña, si no tuviera prisa, le digo todo lo que estoy pensando."

The woman's stunned expression was almost worth it, but

Yaneriz stopped herself from going further. It wasn't worth the energy. She had bigger things to deal with than trading insults with some stranger.

Taking a deep breath, she let the tension roll off her shoulders. *Focus, Yani. You're here for Amaya, not this.*

Once outside the plane, Yaneriz's boots echoed against the mildly glossy floor of the terminal. She scanned the crowd, her eyes taking in the reunion scenes she'd captured countless times as a photographer—faces filled with dread, hope, and happiness, shifting between their phones and the baggage claim.

Would she feel the same when she finally saw Amaya? It had been nearly a year since they last saw each other in person. Sure, they'd FaceTime, but it wasn't the same. Amaya's stationing at Fort Hood had kept her away from home, even during the holidays, with one obligation after another always pulling her away.

Just as a pang of guilt over their distance washed over her, Yaneriz's gaze caught on a pair of familiar brown eyes. She blinked, momentarily distracted by the man's soft, bountiful curls. How are his curls like that? She thought, a flicker of jealousy crossing her mind.

A few minutes later, Yaneriz reached the car rental counter, and she knew then if there was a devil, they lived here because ever since she landed, she has had nothing but distractions. A woman with braids smiled at her—dimples, full lips, sun-tilted eyes. For a few seconds, Yaneriz felt her heart rate spike. The woman was stunning, and Yaneriz felt her resolve waver.

Goddess, get a grip, she thought, wiping her hands on her jeans. She couldn't afford any more of these detours. Not when Amaya needed her.

"One-week rental, please," Yaneriz said, clearing her throat as she refocused on the task at hand.

AS YANERIZ CIRCLED the parking lot, looking for the exit, she spotted the same guy with the perfect curls from earlier. An olive-green duffle bag sat by his foot, and he kept glancing at his phone, clearly waiting for someone. The humidity here was far more intense than El Paso's dry heat—his curls were bound to frizz up soon.

Slowing the car, she lowered her passenger window. "Need a ride?"

The guy squinted at her, suspiciously.

Yaneriz raised a hand. "I promise, not a serial killer."

A slow grin spread across his face. "Neither am I."

Yaneriz smirked, her voice laced with sarcasm. "No offense, but you need to gain weight before considering serial killing."

His eyes widened for a second before he burst out laughing. "None taken. My mom's always pushing food on me. I eat, I just don't hold on to it."

He spread his arms, mock-inspecting his lanky frame.

"Enjoy it while you can. And stay out of the serial killing business," Yaneriz quipped before changing the subject. "I'm heading to the base to surprise my sister, so…"

The guy leaned down, extending his hand inside the car. "I'm Luis. My ride was supposed to pick me up, but he's ghosting me. So, no way I'm leaving my car with him again."

"Ouch," Yaneriz winced sympathetically. "I can drop you wherever you need to go."

"Can you get on base?" he asked, sounding hopeful.

Yaneriz pressed her lips together, thinking for a moment before grinning. She reached out to shake his hand. "Hi, I'm Yaneriz, and I can try."

Pulling back, she flashed her driver's license with a playful wave. "See?"

Luis chuckled, opening the back door to toss in his duffle before sliding into the front seat. "You're not military, I take it?"

"Nope. But my sister is," Yaneriz said. "You don't mind, do you?"

She hadn't really thought through how she'd get on base. It had crossed her mind that she might end up pleading with the security guards or asking them to check on Amaya at her job, but this was easier.

After driving to the registration gate, Luis got Yaneriz a temporary pass to access the base. She had three days which was more than enough to go to Amaya's work and get proof of life and go back to El Paso.

Once they got to Luis's place, he gave her a quick nod before hopping out with his duffle bag. Yaneriz followed the blue dot on her GPS.

As she neared her destination, she spotted a massive horse statue mid-swing, rechecked her map, and knew she'd found Amaya's workplace.

CHAPTER
FIVE

IN THE PARKING LOT, the blue Toyota rental shut off silently. The problem was, it was too quiet. At each light and stop, she thought the rental had died. Back in El Paso, The Hulk made its presence known everywhere she went, rumbling and sputtering like it had a personality of its own. This Toyota, though efficient, felt almost eerie by comparison. Still another detour that kept her from focusing on the one thing she came to do: Find Amaya.

So Yaneriz stepped out of the car, locked it and walked towards Amaya's job. Her boots echoed off the tiled floor as she walked through the front door. But, just as she was about to pass, a young soldier, the girl flagged her down. She couldn't be more than twenty or twenty-one and she was mopping the floor like she had two fucks left in her pocket. "Sergeant Alvarez!"

Yaneriz rolled her eyes. You couldn't pay me enough to do housework in the Army, she thought, scanning for another route. But she wasn't fast enough as the girl soldier inched closer, not letting Yaneriz get away.

"Sergeant Alvarez!" the girl repeated, her tone now

carrying a note of hurt, like she was offended by being ignored.

Yaneriz stopped, exhaling as she looked over her shoulder. The girl's name tag read 'Williams,' and she wore a look of disappointment.

Resigned, Yaneriz turned around. "I'm not—" She was about to explain that she wasn't Amaya and was just looking for her sister when Williams cut her off.

"You know, your hair is lavender, right?" Williams said with a hint of sarcasm, pointing at Yaneriz's curls.

Yaneriz jerked her head back, about to snap back with a sarcastic duh, but Williams was faster.

"You must want to be on extra duty like me," Williams said, without waiting for a reply.

Yaneriz blinked, confused. She opened her mouth again to clarify the misunderstanding, but Williams kept going, talking faster than Yaneriz's shutter speed.

"Look, they're not playing here," Williams said, pointing upwards. "Don't mess around with that hair color because even if you are their favorite, if you make them look bad you'll be mopping floors just like me."

Before Yaneriz could reply, a man's voice boomed from behind her. "What the hell?"

Startled, Yaneriz whipped around and almost slipped on the damp floor. A white man with oily brown hair and skin just as pale stared at her, his face scrunched in disbelief.

"You—you can't sign in like that," he said, his voice thick with disdain, but there was something else in his gaze, a look of shock.

Williams, still mopping, sighed and muttered, "I told you."

The man—Roberts, judging by his name tag—narrowed his eyes. "Alvarez, right?"

Before Yaneriz could correct him, Williams sucked her teeth. "Sergeant Roberts, you act like you haven't driven her and LTC Thompson around a dozen times. You know who she is."

Yaneriz stared at Williams and then at Roberts, unsure of how to proceed. That's when she felt it—a prickle at the back of her neck, like someone was watching her.

—Play along,—said a voice in her head, one that sounded exactly like La Doña.

Yaneriz's breath hitched. How did she hear her grandmother's voice? A voice that is no longer living and hasn't been living for seven years? Yaneriz looked around half expecting to see La Doña, half expecting to be the target of a tasteless prank. But the only thing she spotted were Roberts' confused eyes on her.

Fine, she thought, bringing her attention back to the room before the stranger thinks she had lost her mind. *I'll play along*.

Straightening her posture, Yaneriz placed her hands behind her back like Amaya showed her when recounting what basic training and AIT had been like for her. The movement pulled on her shoulders, the military stance foreign and uncomfortable. But she made herself stand tall.

"Yes, Alvarez," she said, echoing their shared last name and what Amaya was called in the Army.

Roberts raised an eyebrow, clearly not convinced. "I was going to show you your leave form upstairs. You've got two more days, so I've been holding onto it. But if you're back now, I guess you can sign in."

Williams shook her head, still mopping. "Girl, don't do it."

Roberts shot Williams a glare. "You still haven't finished the third floor. Unless you want to stay here longer..."

Williams rolled her eyes and mumbled, "Shit."

"Four more hours of extra duty, Williams," Roberts said with a smirk.

"Fuck this," Williams grumbled, yanking the mop bucket toward the stairwell before disappearing.

"Make that six," Roberts said before turning back to Yaneriz. His smirk deepened. "Let's go to your desk, Alvarez."

A chill crept up Yaneriz's spine, sweat pooling at the back of her neck. She opened her mouth, trying to think of the right Army lingo for vacation, but nothing came. Her brain churned, too scrambled from the flight and the stress. She shoved her hands into her back pockets, trying to appear calm, but when she noticed Roberts watching her closely, she pulled them back out.

—Leave. The word is leave,—La Doña's voice whispered in her mind, cutting through her haze.

"Leave," Yaneriz blurted, catching herself before Roberts could gloat. "I've been on leave."

"Exactly," Roberts said with a wink that made her skin crawl. "You should've stayed home. No need to come back here then."

"I forgot something on my desk," Yaneriz said, forcing her posture to stay rigid.

"Girl, you don't even work in this building," Yaneriz heard Williams whisper above her which told her the girl was still hanging around.

Yaneriz looked up and confirmed it. Her gaze bounced from Williams to Roberts. Between the ragged white dude and the Black Woman, she believed the Black Woman.

"I'll follow you," Roberts said, pushing her to go through with the charade she and La Doña and had gotten herself into and she couldn't back out.

CHAPTER
SIX

THERE WERE ten steps to get to the second floor. Yaneriz counted each one as she climbed.

"I didn't know you were into photography," Roberts said from behind her, his voice oozing with false curiosity.

Yaneriz tapped her camera bag without thinking. She had a habit of taking it everywhere. She wrung her hands, glancing over her shoulder. "My sister got it for me," she said.

"Is that right?" Roberts asked, but there was no real question in his tone.

She looked up the stairwell. Williams had disappeared, and now it was just her and Creepy Roberts. Her eyes flicked between the second-floor door and the third-floor landing. Amaya hadn't told her where exactly she worked; she just said she worked here.

Fifty-fifty shot she could get the floor where her sister works right, she thought, chewing on her bottom lip.

"You forgot your own office?" Roberts' tone was condescending, revealing he knew she didn't know where to go. The itch to punch him surged.

Instead, she took a steadying breath and grabbed the second-floor door handle. The sharp scent of Pine-Sol hit her nostrils as Roberts slid past her and into the second floor.

"You have a sister?" His voice lingered too close, creeping in her ear. Every nerve in her body screamed in discomfort.

"I'm just getting my things," Yaneriz said, louder than necessary to steady her voice. She thought about pushing past him, but there was no guarantee she'd guess which door was Amaya's office. Reluctantly, she followed him.

"Let me show you something first. Then you can grab your stuff," he said, glancing back with a sly grin.

The squeak of his boots echoed through the empty hallway. A sudden chill swept over her, making her want to hug herself tighter. Roberts glanced over his shoulder again, winking at her. Heat rose from her stomach to her head, the anger brewing fast.

I'd mop the floor with his head if I could, she thought, stopping dead in her tracks.

Roberts noticed her hesitation and stopped, too. "You coming?"

Her instincts screamed to turn and run, but she reminded herself, *this is Amaya's job. If I'm going to find anything out, it'll be here. Besides, the voice said to play along.*

With a slow breath, Yaneriz pushed forward. No matter how much Roberts creeped her out, she knew this was where she needed to be. Maybe it was instinct. Maybe it was that shared pain she felt in her chest earlier today. Either way, she pressed on. "Okay."

Roberts led them into another hallway, and a glass wall and door with a dark wooden frame came into view. Army stickers plastered the door, and behind it, a wall of fame boasted photos of soldiers standing stiffly in uniform. Bold red letters spelled out 'The Provider Battalion' above the wall.

Amaya had sent her selfies here when she first arrived. But now, with the lump in her throat tightening, Yaneriz wondered why everything had gone so quiet between them.

As she passed through the doorway, the smell shifted from the sharp Pine-Sol to something different: air-conditioning, ink, and paper. It smelled clean, but in a way that made her feel dirty.

—It's not. It's not clean,—the voice of La Doña whispered, cutting through the quiet.

"That's all you're going to say?" Yaneriz whispered back, exasperated.

Roberts turned, giving her a puzzled look.

Yaneriz waved it off. "Nope. Nothing."

Roberts darted toward an office behind a tall reception desk. "Stay here," he said before disappearing inside.

Yaneriz caught the muffled sound of his voice. "I have someone you should meet, sir."

Whatever was said next must have hit hard, because Roberts' neck and ears turned beet-red. Yaneriz bit the inside of her cheek, pitying him for a moment—until she remembered how he had made her feel. How every word out of Roberts' mouth felt wrong, twisted.

Screw him. She took her pity back.

With a huff, whoever was inside the office shoved Roberts aside and stepped out. The man's face turned ghost-white. He had that look—someone fighting off age with hours at the gym.

Forty-eight, maybe, Yaneriz guessed, sizing him up like she did with the old heads in the gym.

His thinning blond hair was buzzed short, giving him that GI Joe look. But it was his eyes that tripped her up. His cold blue stare sent a shiver down her spine, making her want to bolt.

But she stood her ground.

The man cleared his throat and when Yaneriz looked at him, she knew he didn't have anything blocking his throat but wanted to get her attention and wanted her to know he was important; powerful.

Yaneriz held her breath, unsure whether to stay or run. Something about people with refined noses rubbed her the wrong way. After years of photographing faces, she knew the straighter the nose, the worse the person. Conceited, narcissistic, or worse. She clenched her hands into fists, squaring her stance.

Then a door opened.

Another man emerged from the office, his features more familiar. Yaneriz's eyes flicked to his name tag—Gonzales. The warmth of his coffee-brown eyes, so like her ancestors, contrasted with their hardened expression.

"You're out of uniform, soldier," Gonzales said flatly.

The GI Joe guy—Thompson, she guessed—smirked, his cold blue eyes scanning over her with a dismissive sweep before returning to his office.

Burr. Thompson's last stare sent a shiver danced up and down her spine. She was on edge. *Get a grip Yaneriz,* she thought to herself.

"Man, I tell you. This new generation," Gonzales muttered, shaking his head.

Yaneriz lifted her chin, but the room felt heavy with the suffocating weight of toxic masculinity.

"The Army might have approved a lot of things, but pink hair ain't one of them," Gonzales said in a smug tone.

"It's lavender," Yaneriz corrected, pushing the shakiness out of her voice.

Fire ignited in Gonzales's eyes. "You want to correct me now?"

Behind him, Roberts' smirked screamed 'gotcha way' as he disappeared into Thompson's office.

Outside on her own with Gonzales, the older man stepped closer, causing Yaneriz to take a step back. She wanted to run but refused to give him the satisfaction.

"Damn, how much did you eat on leave? I should have you taped." His gaze raked her body.

"Muscle weighs more than fat," Yaneriz responded, her voice trembling slightly.

Shit, she thought as fear filtered through her body.

Ponte fuerte, her grandmother urged in her mind.

For once, Yaneriz was grateful for her grandmother's presence, even if La Doña wasn't offering much else. Still, the smell of tobacco dip, sweat, and Gonzales' machismo found its way into her nostrils, unnerving her and making her want to vomit.

"I'm giving you two days to get your shit together," Gonzales barked, turning on his heel.

As soon as he moved, the oppressive cloud of his presence lifted, and Yaneriz could finally breathe again.

But Gonzalez stopped, glanced over his shoulder and said, "You'll be the perfect candidate to supervise the extra duty soldier."

Roberts emerged from Thompson's office, his smug grin still plastered on his face.

"Hey, Sergeant Roberts," Gonzales said, "We won't need you much longer if Sergeant Alvarez keeps it up. You'll be off the hook soon, then."

Gonzales clapped Roberts on the back with a bro-slap before walking off.

Roberts chuckled. "Sounds good, Sergeant Major."

Yaneriz shot a narrow-eyed glare at Roberts—the creep—before turning to leave. She wanted—no, she needed to run away from here.

"Wait," Roberts called after her.

Fighting back a fresh wave of irritation, and pushing down her instincts, screaming at her to leave, Yaneriz turned.

"I've got it right here," Roberts said, holding out a form. "Told you I had it."

Yaneriz shook her head. This is what I'm getting from this whole mess? A piece of paper. She couldn't believe it. Reluctantly, she walked over to take it, hoping for something—anything—that might help her.

As soon as her fingers touched the paper, Roberts said, "Wait, I need to make a copy."

Yaneriz raised an eyebrow. *Is this guy serious?* His eyes lingered on Yaneriz longer than she would like. She couldn't take it any longer. Everything was suffocating her. She handed the form back to him careful not to let their fingers touched. "I'll be outside."

She was done with this place at least for now. She could come back when Thompson, Roberts and Gonzales were gone or occupied. Something told her Williams paid more attention than she let on and could give her more information than any of the men lingering upstairs. But for now, she needed to go. The machismo-laced air in this building was choking her and perhaps her sister had already come back and was in fact relaxing in her apartment gearing up to come back again to this hell. Afterall, why would Amaya do this to herself? Why would she work with people like this? Had she pushed her sister into this? Had their childish competitions pushed her sister to prove herself here?

"They don't make Staff Sergeants like they used to, huh?" Gonzales' voice echoed as she left, and Yaneriz couldn't get out of there fast enough.

CHAPTER
SEVEN

YANERIZ LET the door slam behind her. She leaned back against the cold tile wall outside of the carpeted office space, trying to steady herself. Nothing about this situation felt right. Her stomach clenched and growled, reminding her she hadn't eaten all day. Killeen was an hour ahead of El Paso, and it was almost seven. By now, she'd usually be home from the gym, sitting down to dinner.

But these folks? They were still here like the day had just started. The hard splash of a mop hitting the floor echoed in the distance, reminding her that it wasn't just toxicity here. Williams was still around and knowing another woman was nearby brought a small measure of comfort.

Still Yaneriz wondered, *What are they all doing here this late?*

Muffled footsteps and the sound of a door closing pulled her attention. She straightened as Roberts emerged, a sly smile on his face. The cold air from the carpeted workspace seeped out, brushing her face just before the door clicked shut behind him.

"See, I told you," Roberts said, handing her a piece of paper. "Wait two days before you come back. That'll give you time to settle."

Yaneriz narrowed her eyes at him. *That's not what you said downstairs*, she thought, but kept her mouth shut. She didn't want to prolong the interaction.

Roberts extended the paper, and she snatched it from him, turning on her heel to leave. The air in the stairwell was warmer, and the sound of footsteps following her made her bolt down the first flight.

"If you want, I can help you out," Roberts called after her.

Yaneriz stopped, turning slowly, her scowl deepening. "Help me with what?"

"Your hair. Pretending to be a soldier. I have ten years of experience," he said, his tone dripping with false sincerity, like a salesman hawking a lemon.

Her heart pounded, and without a second thought, she dashed down the stairs. "Get the fuck away from me, you creep!"

"I know you're not her!" he shouted after her.

Yaneriz shoved the paper into her back pocket. She didn't trust him, and if it came down to it, she was ready to fight.

Roberts took a step forward.

She backed up.

"I already told you. I just want to help," he insisted raising his hand to show his innocence.

Yaneriz kept her distance, stepping down another stair, her eyes locked on him. Something was off about Roberts that was clear to her; he was that one creep who, knowing they had something over someone, would use it to get whatever favors they wanted. But she wouldn't let him know he was right. She will be Amaya until he can pull off a DNA test, saying otherwise.

"Seriously. I think something happened to her," he said, his voice dropping in urgency.

Her hand hovered near the exit, fingers brushing the cold metal crash bar. She hesitated. A door slammed shut above them, and they both looked up.

"I'm done with the third floor," Williams's voice echoed from above.

"You're still here until 0200," Roberts shot back, his tone dripping with authority.

Yaneriz heard Williams mutter a curse under her breath. The hollow hallway carried every sound, confirming what she already knew—Williams had been there before she slammed the door.

"Roger, Sergeant," Williams replied, her frustration clear. Her eyes met Yaneriz before she dipped the mop in the bucket and started rolling the bucket forward.

Yaneriz's attention snapped back to Roberts. They stood there, watching each other, tension crackling in the air. Her fingers tightened on the crash bar, her body tensing as the door above them opened. The wheels on the mop bucket creaked as they rolled and Williams hummed. Her voice laced with a strange caution that quickened Yaneriz's pulse. "People like to play dumb ... but they'll hurt you when you're done," she sang.

"Oh, shut up," Roberts snapped.

The humming quieted as the door above shut closed. Yet Yaneriz's throat closed with fear. *Was Williams trying to tell me something?*

"Let me help you," Roberts whispered, his voice urgent, almost pleading, taking her out of her reveille.

Yaneriz's jaw clenched, noticing how close Roberts had gotten to her. She shook her head instinctively and pushed the door open, separating them. Her face betrayed nothing, but inside her mind, a debate raged. That's why he rubbed her the wrong way; he was the kind of dude with no personal space and got friendly too fast.

Roberts sighed heavily, his shoulders sagging in defeat. He reached into his pocket and pulled out a lime green sticky note, extending it toward her. "You're going to need this."

Yaneriz hesitated, her eyes narrowing as she considered

the note. Finally, she snatched it from his fingers, tucking it into the folded form in her back pocket without breaking eye contact. She didn't trust him. Not for a second.

Roberts gestured toward the exit. "Go ahead."

She pushed the door further open, stepping to the side, keeping herself out of his path. She'd be damned if she let him get close to her again.

—Don't trust him—her Abuela's voice whispered in her ear.

I'm not, Yaneriz thought, her grip tightening on the door handle.

As Roberts passed by, the nerve pulsing in his cheek gave him away—he was agitated. His hair, stuck together in chunks, looked dirty, or maybe it was just over-gelled. Yaneriz wasn't about to find out. The wave of Axe body spray that followed him clawed at her nostrils, making her fight back a sneeze.

I don't trust you, she thought, her eyes locked on the back of his head as he walked ahead. The distance between them felt like the only safety she had

CHAPTER
EIGHT

IN THE PARKING LOT, finally able to breathe, Yaneriz leaned against her rental car. The cool metal felt grounding, but her mind raced.

"How're you getting into her apartment?" Roberts's voice cut through her thoughts.

Yaneriz squared her chin. "With my key. The key to my apartment."

Roberts scoffed. "You don't even sound convincing."

"Fuck off. If you follow me—"

"What? You gonna call the police and tell them you're impersonating a soldier and trespassing on government property?"

Yaneriz's stomach twisted. She didn't trust the cops, and she sure didn't trust base security. "I'm telling them my sister is missing."

"I thought you were Sergeant Alvarez." His voice dripped with mockery.

Ignoring him, Yaneriz unlocked her car, slipped in, and locked the doors. "If I see you following me, I'll call them," she snapped.

But her mistrust for law enforcement must have shown on

her face, because Roberts smirked. He knew she wouldn't. Her hands trembled as she gripped the steering wheel, trying to steady her breath. The tires squealed as she made a sharp turn out of the parking lot.

Her heart hammered, her thoughts spiraled as she drove through town, eyes glued to the rearview mirror. Once she was sure Roberts wasn't following, Yaneriz punched in her sister's address into the GPS.

Twenty minutes and three left turns later, she arrived at Amaya's apartment complex. The sky above was painted with streaks of rebel reds and pinks, the last light of the sun fading behind the buildings. Yaneriz double-checked her mirrors before stepping out.

A man pushing a stroller gave her a sideways glance, tugging down the stroller's visor as if she were some threat. Yaneriz rolled her eyes. *What, because I've got ripped jeans, worn boots, and lavender hair? Get over yourself.*

With a shrug, she passed him and rushed up the stairs to 209A. There should've been a Trinetta Variegated Schefflera hanging by the door with a false bottom. It was Amaya's favorite plant, and Yaneriz had given her the pot with a hidden key compartment for "just in case" moments—just like this.

But the plant was missing.

"What happened?" she muttered under her breath, her heart sinking.

She pulled out her phone, hoping for a message, a missed call, anything from Amaya. Nothing. *Maybe she's here. Maybe she's back,* she thought, knocking on the door. Her eyes darted to the nearby windows, expecting to see someone peeking out from behind curtains or blinds, but nothing. The complex was quiet, save for the sounds of children refusing to sleep, the clatter of dishes, and faint music from a distant apartment.

Yaneriz pulled her lock-picking kit from her bag. She'd bought it after her landlord charged her $50 for getting locked out, determined never to let that happen again. Now, she was glad for the skill. The lock was like hers—simple. She inserted the wrenches, gently applying pressure until she felt the pins give. The lock clicked open.

As she stepped inside, Amaya's favorite scent, pink blossoms, hit her like a wave. But something was off. The foyer was too clean, too… empty. Her boots echoed as she stepped into the living room. Gray couches sat in neat rows, the glass-and-wood coffee table pristine, with a stack of magazines arranged just so. Teal curtains added a pop of color to an otherwise dreary space.

But the flowers caught her attention. A glass vase held pink-tinted roses with milky white centers, but the water was murky, nearly gone, and the flowers wilted. That didn't make sense. Amaya believed plants had feelings—something she picked up from La Doña. If Amaya knew she wouldn't be back to change the water, she wouldn't have bought them.

With her heart hammering in her chest, Yaneriz whispered, "Something bad happened."

She sat on the couch, drumming her fingers on the coffee table, trying to think. Roberts. His offer to help. It didn't sit right. She didn't trust him. But she couldn't wait two days for Amaya to show up. Not with the ache gnawing at her chest.

Standing up, she passed the small kitchen. The island, which doubled as a dining table, was spotless. The hallway leading to the bedrooms was cold, sterile. Her fingertips scraped against the textured walls, brushing over the unused nails where decorations should've been. Amaya always decorates.

—It's not right—La Doña's voice whispered, confirming her fear.

Anxiety clawed at her. Every shadow felt threatening. She spun in a circle, arms extended, trying to make sense of the emptiness, of her grandmother's cryptic messages since she had started to hear La Doña's voice. But nothing. All she had received from her grandmother were a bunch of words that amounted to nothing. "Just say it! Just goddamn say it already!"

She hated it. Hated how her grandmother never gave a straight answer. Hated those words that haunted her every decision: **You're the oldest. All you two have is each other.**

What did that even mean?

When she was little, the words seemed as vast and incomprehensible as the world itself. To her grandmother, they carried the weight of the universe, some deep truth Yaneriz was supposed to understand. But to Yaneriz, they had been nothing more than a burden, a constant reminder of something she was never prepared for.

What did it mean to be the oldest? What was expected of her, really? To protect? To lead? To sacrifice?

Her grandmother had said it so often, as if Yaneriz was born knowing the answers. But she hadn't. She never had. She'd been a little girl, just like Amaya, trying to make sense of a world that kept taking everything from them.

And now, here she was—once again, standing alone, trying to grasp onto something she didn't fully understand.

Yaneriz wiped furiously at her cheeks, hating how the tears came without permission, without her control. The weight of it all—the loss, the guilt, the anger—pressed down on her, threatening to drown her. She clenched her teeth, her voice breaking as she screamed, "Just say it, Abuela! Tell me exactly what you want from me!"

Yaneriz crumpled to her knees, her voice ragged and strained. Tears streaked down her face, but she didn't care anymore.

"Just say it, Abuela! Just say it!" she screamed into the emptiness, her voice breaking as she felt the weight of her grandmother's presence but heard nothing in return. She wanted to fight it, to scream and shake off the burden. But how could she fight against a ghost? Against the silence?

The words echoed in her head again: **You're the oldest. All you two have is each other.**

Being the oldest hadn't given her all the answers or the strength to bear it all. She didn't know how to be the protector, the guide, the one who kept everything together. Not then. Not now.

She swallowed, her throat raw from the shouting, from the pleading. Her heart ached with guilt, with grief. For all her grandmother's guidance, for all the whispered words in the dark, she had failed. She had failed Amaya. She hadn't been enough.

"Please," she whispered, her voice a fragile thing now, trembling. "Just say it, Abuela. Tell me what you need from me. I don't know what to do anymore."

Her breath hitched, and for a moment, she waited. Waited for her grandmother to appear. Waited for the voice that had always been there, always lingering just beyond reach. But the apartment remained still. The weight of the air pressed down on her, and the only thing that answered her was silence.

Just silence.

Yaneriz hung her head, her body shuddering with the sobs she could no longer hold back. It was the only answer she got. Nothing. No cryptic message. No guidance. No comfort.

She was on her own.

Tears fell from her cheeks, dampening her jeans. She felt emptier than ever, the realization settling into her bones like a cold, unshakable truth.

"Some help you are," she muttered, her voice barely audible, bitter in the hollow silence of the apartment.

The room felt larger now, the quietness swallowing her whole. Yaneriz stared ahead, numb, the last remnants of hope flickering and fading in the shadows.

She was alone.

At that realization, she lifted her head. She needed to check her sister's apartment. She needed to keep going. At the end of the hallway, a door hung ajar. She walked over. It was the bathroom—spotless, untouched, as if no one had been here in weeks. Across from it, the door to what had to be Amaya's bedroom stood slightly open.

The pink blossom scent was stronger here, but there was something else—disinfectant. A heavy smell, lingering in the air like a warning.

Yaneriz's stomach churned. "You're right," she begrudgingly whispered into the room. "Something's wrong."

Amaya never touched bleach. It didn't align with her hippy tendencies—always opting for eco-friendly, natural cleaners over the heavy-duty stuff found in supermarkets. That's who Amaya was, the kind of person who believed in making the world better, one vinegar and lemon concoction at a time. Yaneriz had never quite understood why her free-spirited, nature-loving sister would join the Army. It seemed contradictory, unless, in some idealistic, warped way, Amaya thought she could change the system from the inside. Still, regardless of whether she got the reason behind her sister's enlistment, one thing was certain—Amaya would never have allowed bleach in her home.

So why did the entire apartment reek of it?

Yaneriz's chest tightened as suspicion turned into certainty. She rushed to the kitchen and flung open the cabinet beneath the sink. Sure enough, there they were—the reusable bottles filled with Amaya's usual homemade cleaning solutions: vinegar, water, lemon rinds. Exactly what she expected.

No bleach.

Her heart thudded in her chest as she stared at the familiar bottles. If Amaya hadn't cleaned this place, then who had?

With shaking hands, Yaneriz pulled the lime-green note from her back pocket. She stared at Roberts' number, every fiber of her being screaming for answers. She could meet him in the morning, in plain sight and validate whatever he gave her with Williams. That plan made the knot in Yaneriz stomach from the thought of talking to Roberts again, ease.

—Don't—La Doña's voice whispered, stopping her in her tracks.

Yaneriz stood still, arms at her sides. "Don't what?"

Silence again.

"Don't what?" she shouted, spinning in another circle, searching for some clue, some answer.

But nothing came. She couldn't depend on the voice, just like she couldn't depend on the cops. Memories of New York flooded her mind—the time her roommate had vanished without a trace. She remembered going to the police, frantic, only to be dismissed with the standard line: "Wait it out, maybe she went to a party or needed space." They didn't care, not until her roommate's wealthy parents from Florida got involved, throwing around the weight of their money and status. By the time the police finally acted, it was too late. The damage had been done. After that, Yaneriz packed up her life, moved to El Paso, and swore she'd never have another roommate.

Now, standing here, the same dread gnawing at her, she knew it would be the same story. No one would listen. They wouldn't believe her about Amaya. They'd dismiss her, tell her to wait, to be patient—just like before.

And this time, she couldn't afford to wait.

"No," she said, shaking her head. "I'm not waiting. I'm not depending on them."

Her hand brushed the crumpled paper in her back pocket. She sighed and pulled out the lime-green sticky note with Roberts' number.

THE SOUND of grinding coffee beans pulled Yaneriz's attention to the counter. Chrome-finished espresso machines gleamed under the morning light, and her reflection stared back from the mirror behind them. She'd only managed two hours of sleep before her mind told her to get up and keep going. It was 5:00 a.m. when she texted Roberts, and by 5:10 a.m., he had responded. Now, at 10:00 a.m., she was groggy and wired all at once.

When Yaneriz first got to Santo's Coffee Shop, she had moved to a table at the back of the shop to give her a better view of everyone who came. Being a photographer meant she enjoyed people watching. But this joy left her as she watched Roberts's arrival, thirty minutes after hers. Wrinkled Army camouflage, unkempt greasy hair, and circles under his eyes that matched the brown in his uniform, had revulsion bubbling up inside Yaneriz's throat. In comparison, Amaya had looked radiant in her uniform when she came home after basic training. Despite being a little on the skinny side and solemn from finding out La Doña had passed, her sister shined like a star.

Filled with curiosity, Yaneriz watched as Roberts leaned

over the counter to put his order with the barista. Flor scrounged her nose, and instinctively leaned back, clearly uncomfortable when he got too close. Unbeknownst to the barista's reaction to him, Roberts turned back and grinned at Yaneriz. Once he paid for his order, he sauntered over the table with unwarranted confidence.

"You texted," he said, sliding into the seat across from her.

"Obviously," Yaneriz replied, rolling her eyes to mask her unease.

Roberts unlocked his phone, scrolling until he found something. He turned the screen toward her. "This is what I've got."

The warmth drained from Yaneriz's face at the sight of a text message from her sister asking for help. Her hands clenched into fists on the table. "Why didn't you help Amaya?"

At the mention of Amaya's name, Roberts's eyes avoided Yaneriz's. His smile faded too quickly.

"I was about to. See?" Roberts pointed at the subsequent message on the screen, his finger hovering over a text thread. "But then she stopped texting."

"Why didn't you tell me that yesterday?" Yaneriz snapped.

"There are too many eyes and ears in that building. You can't trust everyone. And afterward, it didn't seem like you wanted to talk to me."

Because you're a fucking creep, she thought. Her jaw tightened.

—Listen to me. Don't trust him—La Doña whispered, her voice firm in Yaneriz's ear.

I don't, she thought back, wishing La Doña could feel the intensity of her distrust.

"Are you okay?" Roberts asked, his tone suddenly concerned.

"I'm fine," she said sharply, her cheeks burning.

Flor, the barista, appeared with their drinks. She set down

a coffee mug in front of Roberts and a small espresso in front of Yaneriz.

"Thank you," Yaneriz said, grateful for the interruption.

"Of course," Flor replied, giving her arm a reassuring squeeze before walking away.

"I take it you don't like guys," Roberts said, raising an eyebrow.

Yaneriz shot him a withering glare. "I take it you don't know how to mind your own business."

Roberts raised his hands in surrender. "Okay, okay." He cleared his throat. "Look, I know where she was last."

Yaneriz's eyes snapped to his. "How do you know that?"

"Right before her leave, your sister had a recon mission."

"A what?"

"She had to check out a location for training. It's out in the woods, part of the training area. She'd only been there once before and didn't want to get lost, so I gave her the grid coordinates. She shared her location with me in case anything happened. And three days ago, I checked—her location was still on, and she was in the same area."

Yaneriz's blood ran cold. "And you didn't tell anyone? No one bothered to look for her?"

Roberts winced. "It doesn't work like that here."

Yaneriz's fists tightened. It had been a month since she'd last spoken to her twin. Amaya had changed since joining the Army, but one thing had never changed—Amaya was always good at finding places. Their grandmother used to say that Yaneriz inherited their father's temper, while Amaya got his sense of direction. He had driven buses in the Dominican Republic and taxis in New York City before GPS existed. He only had to visit a place once, and he'd know how to get there. Amaya had that same knack. So, if she was still in the same place, something was very wrong. Still there was a chance Amaya was out there, lost and waiting for help.

"Where's the spot?" Yaneriz asked, her voice icy.

Roberts leaned back. "It's out in the training area. You can't go there."

Yaneriz downed her espresso in one sharp gulp. "The address."

Roberts hesitated, narrowing his eyes at her. The look reminded her of yesterday when he saw right through her.

A tense silence hung between them. Yaneriz's hands shook from the caffeine, but she kept her gaze steady. Finally, Roberts scrolled through his phone again and showed her the screen.

The blue dot on the map pulsed like a beacon, hovering over a remote area.

Yaneriz clicked on it. An info box with an address popped up. She swiftly snapped a picture. "Thanks."

"Wait, you're not going to finish your coffee?" Roberts asked.

"I did," Yaneriz said as she stood, walking toward the door.

Roberts followed her out, his steps too close for comfort. To her annoyance, when Yaneriz opened the cafe's door she noticed Roberts had parked right next to her. As she reached for her key, it snagged on a loose thread in her jacket. She yanked it, but the key slipped from her grasp and clattered to the ground.

As she bent to pick it up, a loud honk startled her upright.

She spun around, half-expecting it to be Roberts.

But it was some guy in a souped-up Subaru, revving his engine like he was in a Fast and Furious movie.

"We get a lot of those here," Roberts said, his voice too close.

Yaneriz glanced behind her, and sure enough, Roberts was standing there, hat on but cocked back, making him look even more raggedy, a thin smile stretched across his face.

"I still don't trust you," Yaneriz whispered, her voice barely audible as she moved toward her rental.

She unlocked the door. The ping of a text message took her attention.

'Don't trust Roberts,' from a 254-area code.

She threw the phone in her passenger seat, determined to get as far away as possible from him. But as she pulled the seatbelt across her chest, she noticed something—Roberts was standing outside her passenger door, staring into her backseat.

Her heart raced. She'd heard the stories—women being kidnapped or strangled by someone hiding in the back of their car. Her breath caught in her throat as she whipped her head around, scanning the backseat, fists clenched, ready to defend herself.

But there was nothing.

The passenger door slammed shut, and almost immediately, pain exploded in the back of her skull. The world spun, her vision darkening like a curtain slowly drawing closed.

Fuck was the last thought she had before everything went black.

CHAPTER
TEN

YANERIZ LAY ON HER SIDE, the hard metal of the trunk pressing into her ribs, each bump in the road jostling her sore limbs. Her head throbbed, but her thoughts were far from here. She squeezed her eyes shut, willing herself to stay calm, breathe through the pain, and let the panic subside.

A memory flickered in the darkness behind her eyelids—a hot summer afternoon in the D.R. She and Amaya had spent the whole day by the river, skipping stones and laughing like the world was theirs. But before that, she had almost drowned. The day before, one of their cousins had played too rough in the river at Samaná, pulling her under, and Yaneriz had swallowed too much water. She remembered the moment her feet had lost touch with the riverbed, and terror had consumed her until their cousin had pulled her out, laughing like it had been a joke.

For Yaneriz it was not a joke, almost drowning became a nightmare. She thought Amaya had sense that because it had been her who fought their cousin. Her who had gotten in trouble that day. It was also her who got her back to the river.

The next day, Amaya begged Yaneriz to come back to the

river, afraid that fear would win if she didn't face it. That's when they'd spent the whole day skipping stones.

"Yani got noodle arms!" Amaya had teased, using her nickname for Yaneriz.

Yaneriz had grinned wide, forcing the smile she forced on her face to combat the fear that rushing water was giving her. So, they battled each other close to the water while not being in it. They hurled stones across the water's surface, watching it bounce. Yaneriz's throws were more of a flop. Amaya, on the other hand, seemed to have done that more than once before. This was something she wasn't better than her sister and Yaneriz for once felt good about not being better. Still at her sister's comment Yaneriz had stuck her tongue out and with faux bravado retorted, "Better than you."

The river had been peaceful, their laughter the only sound against the backdrop of the precarious rush of water. Yaneriz longed to return to that moment, when her sister's laughter shielded her from fear. When the only worry was how far the stone would skip. When Amaya's laugh had rung out with joy.

The memory crumbled as the car hit another bump, and she was pulled back into the suffocating darkness of the trunk. Her neck and hip screamed in pain, as if she'd slept in the worst position imaginable. The air was thick with gasoline fumes, the sound of a car engine vibrating around her.

"What the fuck?" she muttered, trying to sit up. Her head banged against something hard. "Coño!"

"Good morning, sleeping beauty," came Roberts' cocky voice from the front.

Hearing him made the last 24 hours flood back. That bastard had knocked her out. Yaneriz rubbed her temples, trying to calm herself, but no matter how hard she tried, waves of anger rolled over her.

"So, it was you!" she yelled, her voice filled with rage.

"I can't hear you!" Roberts called out in a sing-song tone, like they were two friends on a road trip.

"Bullshit!"

"Should've stayed in Hell Paso taking stupid pictures," Roberts taunted, his voice edging into something more sinister. The maniacal undertone made her stomach turn.

Yaneriz pulled at her wrists, but the duct tape held firm. She twisted her body, trying to maneuver toward the trunk door. The car bounced, and her hip slammed into something hard and metal. Pain shot through her entire body, making her scream.

Minutes passed, and the excruciating pain morphed into a dull throb. Her breath came in short, shallow gasps.

—Respira, mi niña—her grandmother's voice whispered.

Despite the pain, a small smile tugged at Yaneriz's lips. La Doña always said that, as if breathing fixed everything. Fixed losing parents, growing up too fast, being abandoned by the uncles who were supposed to care for her.

Then a wisp of light appeared before her eyes. It wasn't blinding, just a gentle glow that somehow brought calm. Her breath steadied.

—Yo sé, pero me tienes que creer, todo va estar bien, mi cicloncito—her grandmother whispered again.

For the first time, Yaneriz felt a shift within herself. Maybe, just maybe, La Doña had been trying to help all along, in whatever way she could—whether in life or death. *Who really knows what ghosts can or can't do?* That thought softened her heart towards her grandmother, towards the cryptic ways La Doña had always pushed her. Perhaps there had been guidance in those riddles, after all.

Once her thoughts cleared, a pressing question emerged: *Where is Roberts taking me?*

She pulled her legs back as far as possible and kicked the trunk with all her might.

"Shit!" Roberts cursed, the car swaying back and forth

before coming to a stop. Footsteps crunched on dried leaves outside. The trunk creaked open, and the pale moonlight flooded in, momentarily blinding her.

Roberts stood there, his gaze dangerous. "I should've killed you back there," he muttered.

The regret in his tone sent a chill down Yaneriz's spine.

He glanced at the part of the trunk she had kicked, raising an eyebrow. "That's coming out of your bill," he said dryly.

Her eyes darted behind him, searching for clues— anything to give her a sense of where she was. The blue bumper of the car and the shape of the headlights told her what she needed to know. It was her rental. His comment about the bill makes sense now, she thought bitterly. But who cares about fees when you're dead?

A morbid smile crossed her lips at the thought of her uncles in the D.R. getting stuck with her bills. That would be some kind of karmic justice.

"You think this is funny?" Roberts asked, leaning closer.

The musty scent that clung to him made her stomach churn. Yaneriz clenched her fists, fury coursing through her. She stared him down, her smile shifting into a grimace.

"After I find my sister," she growled into his ear, "I'm going to kill you."

Roberts huffed. "Yeah, okay."

The trunk slammed shut, and Yaneriz was left in darkness again. Something caught her eye—a faint glow. She shifted her body, wriggling toward it. The emergency latch. Roberts had covered it in tape, probably hoping she wouldn't notice it in the dark.

The car picked up speed. Yaneriz braced herself, pushing her chin forward until the latch brushed against her nose. She waited for it to swing back and bit down on it.

She knew what would happen once she pulled it—she'd have to roll out immediately. Her heart pounded, and pain shot through her body as if warning her of the agony yet to come. She grunted, pushing through the fear.

—Tu lo puedes hacer, mi niña—her grandmother's voice whispered, steady and encouraging.

Yaneriz shook her head, but she clamped her teeth harder around the latch. With a deep breath, she yanked it. The trunk popped open, and a rush of wet, grassy air hit her face. Without hesitation, she rolled out of the car. Her body slammed into the ground with a heavy thud, knocking the wind out of her and sending sharp pain shooting through every bone.

"Coño," she gasped, her voice barely a whisper.

Tiny scratches burned her skin as she lay there, struggling to catch her breath. She craned her neck just in time to see the car speeding away. But relief was short-lived.

The brake lights turned from red to white in the corner of her vision. The car was reversing.

Her heart leaped. Adrenaline surged through her, masking the pain. With her hands still tied, she forced herself to her feet and darted into the woods, pushing deeper until even the pale moonlight couldn't reach her.

LOW-HANGING branches swiped at the cuts on Yaneriz's face, drawing fresh blood. She pushed the limbs away with her shoulders, her hands still bound behind her back. She slowed down as her balance wavered, nearly sending her sprawling to the ground. *Better scratched than unable to get up,* she thought.

"Shit," she heard Roberts mutter, his breath labored and close.

Yaneriz wasn't Army strong like Amaya, but hiking in El Paso's high elevation, hauling photography gear, and doing CrossFit twice a week had given her endurance. Still, Roberts was closing the distance. She crouched low, keeping her movements deliberate, letting the trees obscure her as much as possible.

"She jumped out!" Roberts' voice pierced the night, closer than she'd hoped.

Panic flared as she reached a path devoid of foliage. Her own indented footprints glared at her under the weak moonlight. *If I can see them, so can he.*

"No, no, no," she whispered, heart racing.

Breathing hard, Yaneriz fell to her knees, grabbed a fallen

branch between her teeth, and used it to sweep away her tracks. Every movement sent pain radiating from her bruised hip, but she fought through it even as fear tightened her chest.

"I'm going to find her," Roberts called again, more frustrated this time.

Not if I can help it, Yaneriz thought. The tremble in her hands worsened. She took another step backward, careful not to snap any twigs underfoot. But in an instant, her foot hit nothing but air. Her eyes widened in terror as she teetered on the edge of a drop. She clamped her mouth shut to keep from screaming as she fell.

She landed hard on her back, sliding down the muddy slope. With her hands bound, she turned her body to dig her shoulder into the dirt, trying to slow her descent. Mud seeped into her collar, cold and slick against her skin. She tugged at her taped wrists, but even the mud couldn't weaken the adhesive. *Did Roberts use the whole damn roll?* She wondered with a grim expression.

Above her, branches snapped under someone's weight. Yaneriz glanced up, her breath catching.

"I got her," Roberts said, his voice triumphant.

His silhouette hovered at the top of the hill, his yellowed teeth glinted in the moonlight. He'd discarded his army top and was now in just his brown undershirt, the fabric tight around his paunch. The sight of him filled Yaneriz with a wave of revulsion.

No time for disgust now, she thought. She turned onto her back, pressed her feet into the dirt, and pushed herself down the hill as fast as she could. The incline carried her faster, the branches scraping her skin and ripping at her clothes. When she hit the bottom, her body was slick with mud, her breathing ragged.

Finally, she thought, yanking at the tape again. The mud

and sweat had weakened the adhesive, and she managed to pull her wrists free.

She glanced back at the hill. Roberts was stumbling down it sideways, using branches for balance, but the slick mud was making it difficult for him to stay upright.

Without a second thought, Yaneriz bolted toward the river.

The cold water rushed into her boots, seeping up her legs. She hadn't thought about the river's depth when she ran, but now, waist-deep panic gripped her. I can't swim. She remembered her cousin's game in the water. Her later failed attempts as an adult to learn and how even now, her fear hinged on that one terrifying moment when she almost drowned.

"I got this," she whispered, forcing herself to take deep breaths.

Roberts' hard breathing echoed behind her. He wasn't far.

"I got this," she repeated, louder this time, as she lifted her legs higher through the water. Her voice squeaked, betraying her fear, but she pressed on.

The night and the sound of rushing water filled her with doubt. I know basic swimming, she reminded herself, even as the current pulled at her.

Her foot slipped on a rock, and the water surged up to her chest. Panic rose like bile in her throat. A scream fought to escape, but she swallowed it, lifting her chin to keep from inhaling more river water.

"You don't know how to swim, island girl?" Roberts taunted, his voice laced with condescension as he reached the riverbank.

Yaneriz froze, her breath ragged. That tone—so smug, so dismissive—ignited something in her. She went back to the day Amaya forced her to go back to the river, had forced her to face her fear and with that in mind, she flicked her head to the side, whipping her wet hair out of her face.

"I'm not dying tonight," she growled through clenched teeth.

She pushed forward, ignoring the icy water splashing into her face. Her muscles screamed as she skipped through the river, losing her footing more than once. She swallowed mouthfuls of water and gasped for breath, but she didn't stop. Finally, her feet hit solid ground on the other side.

Her body trembled uncontrollably, whether from the cold or the adrenaline, she couldn't tell. She looked back across the river, her chest heaving.

In the middle of the river, Roberts was swimming sideways, struggling against the current. If it didn't hurt so much to breathe, Yaneriz would have laughed.

And this is why thick girls win, she thought, a small grin creeping across her face.

But she couldn't gloat for long. Ahead of her loomed another steep hill, just as treacherous as the last one. Her thighs burned at the thought of climbing it. She took a shaky breath, ready to push forward when a pair of headlights flashed above, circling near the river.

Hope fluttered in her chest. Someone's here. She forced her body into motion, her legs pumping harder than they ever had before. There was no time for hesitation. Whoever was driving could be her only chance of help.

CHAPTER
TWELVE

ON THE OTHER side of the ridge and out of breath, Yaneriz glanced back. Roberts hadn't even made it halfway up. He had just crossed the river and was doubled over, panting heavily at the bottom. Shaking her head, Yaneriz turned and took off after the jeep that had passed moments before.

"Help!" she called out, waving her hands frantically. "Help!"

The jeep came to a stop.

Relief flooded through her as she jogged the rest of the way. But as she got closer, her heart sank. It wasn't a random jeep—it was a park ranger truck. And sitting in the passenger seat was Amaya's commander, LTC Thompson.

Her breath caught in her throat as Thompson pulled a gun and aimed it squarely at her.

"Park's closed, darling," the heavy-set park ranger in the driver's seat drawled, his Texas accent thick and unsettling.

A million thoughts raced through Yaneriz's mind, each worse than the last. Then, she noticed one of the park ranger's boots hitting the ground, and something clicked.

She remembered the boy from high school who wouldn't

leave Amaya alone. Every day, he pestered her, and every day, she said no. When Yaneriz offered to talk to him, Amaya had refused, wanting to handle it herself. But the day Raul cornered Amaya at the bus stop, Yaneriz knew she had to step in and stop it even if Amaya didn't wanted her to. That day she knocked him flat with a shoulder tackle and Raul never bothered Amaya again.

—Eso mismo. Hazlo. ¡Ahora!—La Doña's voice snapped her back to the present.

Her grandmother's voice jolted her into action. Yaneriz dropped her hands and rammed her shoulder into the jeep's door with all her strength. The sound of bones crunching echoed in the air. The park ranger's foot, which had been dangling out of the jeep, now hung at a sickening angle. He cursed and collapsed back toward Thompson, whose gun went off with a deafening crack.

Yaneriz didn't wait to see if the bullet had hit her. She ran.

Her breath came in ragged gasps as she patted her body, her mind flashing back to the war documentaries she had watched to understand Amaya better. Veterans had spoken about how adrenaline could mask pain, how they didn't even realize they'd been shot until much later. Yaneriz frantically checked her arms, torso, and legs for blood, but all she felt was sweat and nerves.

—Corre, Yaneriz. Corre— her grandmother urged.

She pumped her legs harder, every muscle and tendon straining as she tore through the woods. After what felt like an eternity but was only ten minutes, she stumbled to a stop in front of a small cabin. She darted around the property, peeking through windows, praying to find someone—anyone —inside. But the place was empty.

Desperation clawed at her. She ran to the back door and patted her pockets for her lock-picking kit, but Roberts had emptied them when he took her bag. Anger surged through her veins as she stooped, picking up a rock. *Old-school it is,* she thought.

Raising the rock to smash the window, she hesitated. If Thompson and the park ranger were close enough, they'd hear the sound of breaking glass. Yaneriz slowed her breathing, listening to the night for any sign of pursuit. An owl hooted in the distance, making her jump, but the night remained still.

With one swift motion, she tapped the window with the rock's pointy end. The glass cracked. She pushed her elbow into the weak spot and shattered it. Ignoring the pain, she crawled through the broken window and into the dark cabin.

She moved cautiously, her hands out in front of her, groping through the darkness. Her head still throbbed from when Roberts had knocked her out, and she wasn't sure she could trust what she was feeling or seeing. Just get to the kitchen, she told herself, hoping to find something—anything —to defend herself.

Growing up, Yaneriz had always been in charge of cutting up whatever animal her grandmother brought home. More often than not, it was a recently unalived chicken, its neck freshly wrung by La Doña's weathered hands. Yaneriz could still remember the weight of the bird, its feathers hastily plucked, and the expectation on her grandmother's face as she presented it to her, demanding that she clean and cut it up. While Amaya had been in charge of cleaning the kitchen afterward, Yaneriz's duty had always involved the blade. She knew what a knife could do—to flesh and bones. Every cut, every crack of bone beneath the sharp edge had been a lesson to her.

A gun was more lethal, yes. It kept the distance. But a knife? A knife meant being close—too close. Yet, it was better than nothing.

Her fingers brushed against cold metal. A sink. There had to be knives nearby. She needed something, anything.

"Please let me find a knife," she whispered, half praying.

But as she rifled through the drawers, all she found were empty spaces. Not even a spoon. Frustration bubbled over.

"Fuck, fuck, fuck!" she cursed, kicking the cabinet. Pain shot through her toes, making her collapse onto the floor in agony. Tears stung the back of her eyes. I'm going to die in a cheap, unfurnished cabin, and I'll never find my sister.

—¡Párate!—La Doña's voice snapped her out of her self-pity.

Yaneriz reluctantly reached above her, grabbing a drawer handle and pulling herself up. A sudden, blinding light seared her eyes. She had opened a drawer with an automatic night light.

"Coño!" she hissed, slamming it shut.

Outside, the sound of hurried footsteps and hushed voices approached.

"Over there," someone shouted.

Blinking away the spots from the light, Yaneriz felt her way along the counter. She couldn't leave without something to defend herself. Her hand scraped against a block of wood. A knife block. Her fingers closed around a plastic handle, and she pulled out a knife. The metal gleamed faintly in the dim light.

Gripping the knife tightly, she crawled back out through the window. But as soon as her boots hit the ground, someone grabbed her hair and yanked her back. Pain exploded through her scalp as her neck snapped backward. The cold steel of a gun muzzle pressed against her temple.

"You should've stayed in El Paso, Yaneriz," Thompson's voice growled in her ear.

"HELP!" Yaneriz screamed, her voice ragged.

Thompson's arm constricted around her neck like a vice, and the cold muzzle of the gun pressed painfully into the throbbing vein in her temple. Yaneriz kicked wildly, her legs flailing behind her, but she couldn't make contact with anything. Stars flickered in front of her eyes as her breath thinned. The click of the gun's safety being disengaged echoed in her ears, and for a split second, Yaneriz felt her spirit leave her body, ready to meet La Doña.

"Your sister gave me problems. You're just as bad. Is it a twin thing? This stubbornness?" Thompson's ragged breath warmed the side of her face.

Yaneriz's eyes fluttered open. If she could hear him, feel his breath—she wasn't dead yet. He hadn't pulled the trigger. Gasping for air, she shoved her elbow back toward him, but he shifted, anticipating her movement.

"Yes, it must be," Thompson continued, his voice detached and annoyed, as though he were dealing with a trivial inconvenience.

The way he said "was" when speaking of Amaya sent a

cold, paralyzing wave through Yaneriz's body. Her heart sank as the horrible realization crept in—he wasn't just referring to Amaya being difficult. He was implying her sister was gone.

"You—" Yaneriz started, her voice hoarse.

Before she could finish, Roberts stumbled into view, his breathless arrival cutting her off.

"I almost had her," Roberts wheezed, still catching his breath.

Thompson clicked his tongue in disgust. "You're worthless."

"I got her here, didn't I?" Roberts whined, his voice grating like a child seeking approval.

Thompson scoffed, but said nothing more.

With her back against Thompson and Roberts looming in front of her, Yaneriz was trapped. Every fiber of her being rejected the hopelessness of her situation, but her options felt limited. She could hardly breathe, her neck pulsed with pain, and her mind reeled with the discovery that Thompson had been involved in hurting her sister. But a flicker of something inside her refused to surrender.

"You had the other twin," Roberts sneered, inching closer, his foul breath making Yaneriz's stomach churn. She fought the urge to shut down, to retreat within herself.

—Ponte fuerte—La Doña's voice whispered, pulling her back from the edge. She was no longer a helpless ten-year-old trapped by two neighbors coercing her to show them her panties. She was an Alvarez woman.

In two swift moves, Yaneriz rammed her elbow hard into Thompson's ribs. The unexpected contact forced him to loosen his grip on her neck, and she slid out of his hold. Gasping for air, she spun and grabbed Roberts by the head, driving her knee into his nose. The sickening crack echoed in the night. She whipped around, slapping Thompson's gun from his grasp.

Her eyes darted to the knife she'd dropped earlier, but it lay too close to Roberts, who was writhing on the ground, blood streaming from his nose. The woods offered a better chance of survival than retrieving the knife and confronting them again. Winded but determined, Yaneriz sprinted toward the tree line.

Her mind raced back to something she'd seen on TikTok from a self-defense creator: If someone is chasing you with a gun, run in a zigzag pattern. Hope surged through her veins at the thought that she may get out of this alive.

But before she could get far, a burning sensation seared through her arm. She screamed, pain ripping through her as warm blood trickled down her skin. Her knees buckled as the weakness crept in.

—Respira mi niña. Respira—La Doña whispered softly in her mind.

Yaneriz managed a small, pained smile at the words. She sucked in a deep breath and pressed her hand against the wound, slowing her pace to a jog as her legs turned to mush. The tree line blurred in the darkness, and the world around her became a maze of shadows.

—Ponle presión, Yaneriz—her grandmother urged.

"I am," she muttered through gritted teeth.

Her feet kicked something solid. She stopped to pat it— rocks. A formation tall enough to hide behind. Glancing back, she saw no movement and slipped behind the rock. Her fingers fumbled with her shirt, wincing as she tore a piece of material off. Like Abuela had done for Amaya when she cut her leg, Yaneriz wrapped the fabric tightly around her arm, putting pressure on the open wound to prevent more blood loss. She fought back tears as waves of pain washed over her.

With her back against the cold stone, Yaneriz looked up at the waning moon barely peeking through the treetops. Tears stung her eyes as her thoughts drifted. She could still feel

Amaya's presence, the familiar pull of their connection lingering in the air.

Amaya...

Memories swirled in her mind, pulling her back to the day she had felt her sister's pain across the distance. Many years later, they had both apologized for their roles in that long-ago accident. From that conversation, Amaya had left her with those last words—**I love you, and it was not your fault.**

Remembering that, Yaneriz whispered into the night, "I love you too."

The sound of footsteps jolted her out of the memory. She bolted upright, heart racing. A flashlight beam whipped across the ground, barely missing her hand as she snatched it back. The light passed, and she crouched lower, her breathing shallow.

"I know you're here," Thompson's voice called out, chilling her to the core.

Where was Roberts? Yaneriz couldn't dwell on that. She gripped a rock she had found and crouched lower. She listened intently to Thompson's footsteps, calculating the distance between them. If he passed her by, she'd have only a few seconds to act.

"Might as well give up," Thompson taunted, his cocky tone setting her nerves on edge. "It won't be as bad if you do."

Yaneriz stifled a huff of anger. She could hear the arrogance in his voice, the self-assurance that made her blood boil. She pressed her hand over her mouth, willing herself to stay silent.

Thompson's footsteps quickened. "Amaya was right. You're the more stubborn one. It must run in the family."

Was. That word echoed in Yaneriz's mind, fueling her rage.

Thompson's outline appeared against the dim moonlight. Yaneriz crouched lower, her legs burning, every breath deliberate and slow.

One.

Two.

Three.

Thompson was just two steps away.

Four.

With light feet, Yaneriz stepped behind him, keeping her movements as quiet as possible.

"Wait, what the—"

Before he could turn, she kicked him in the lower back, hard. The crack of bones told her she had hit him with just the right amount of force. Thompson collapsed to the ground with a heavy thud. Yaneriz didn't hesitate. Straddling his back, she raised the rock high above her head and slammed it down on his skull with all her might.

"You fucking bitch!" Thompson gargled, his voice breaking.

But Yaneriz was beyond hearing him. She brought the rock down again and again, blinded by rage, until no more bones cracked beneath her blows. Her breath came in short, ragged gasps as she finally stopped, her muscles burning and trembling.

"Amaya..." she whispered, her voice breaking.

Pushing away from Thompson's lifeless form, Yaneriz curled into a ball, needing the comfort of a trusting human being but having none. She pulled her knees to her chest. Curled up against her own warmth, her own beating heart, surrounded by death and violence, she let her tears flowed freely. Her tears became sobs, and her body shook with them. Yaneriz whispered her sister's name over and over, as if the chant could bring her back. Her untamed sorrow filled the surrounding air. Knowing that Amaya would never come back, she stared at her hands tainted with the blood of one of the men who took her sister's life away; who made her something so unnatural; a sole twin.

Have I become a monster? Have I become what I killed? Yaneriz asked herself, the question lingering in the privacy of her soul.

But the crunch of leaves behind her shattered the moment. Yaneriz stilled, wiping her eyes on her collar. She didn't know how much time had passed, but she knew someone was there. Holding her breath, she listened.

The footsteps were light, deliberate. Roberts.

La Doña's voice cut through her spiraling thoughts.—Los monstruos no preguntan si son monstruos— *The monsters don't ask if they are monsters.*

Her grandmother's words both sobered and appeased her. It would have to be enough, for now. She couldn't afford to dwell on her conscience—not when the real danger was closing in. That reckoning would have to wait. Whether she made it out alive or not depended on what she did next. Yaneriz shifted her focus entirely to the present. She needed to stop Roberts before he killed her.

Her gaze locked on Thompson's gun lying nearby. Crouching low, she darted toward it just as Roberts came into view.

"You fucking bitch," Roberts growled.

Yaneriz ignored the insult and slid across the ground, her fingers closing around the cold metal. She rolled onto her back, aiming the gun at the shadowy figure approaching her.

"Try me," she said, her voice steady despite her shaking hands.

Roberts froze.

"Hands," she ordered.

Roberts lifted his hands, then lunged.

Yaneriz clicked off the safety. "One more step, and your head will look worse than his."

Roberts backed off; his hands raised higher.

"Drop your phone," she commanded.

He flung the phone away, the light bouncing until it

stopped rolling. Keeping the gun trained on him, Yaneriz grabbed the phone and shoved it into her back pocket.

"You don't know how to use that," Roberts sneered.

"You want to find out?" Yaneriz shot back.

His silence was answer enough.

"Take me to my sister," she said, her voice cold and unwavering.

CHAPTER
FOURTEEN

ROBERTS BROKE the silence when the cabin Yaneriz had broken into came into view.

"Look, just call the police. Please." His voice had lost its smugness, replaced by a tone that was almost desperate.

"No," Yaneriz replied coldly.

"You're not going to like it," he warned, as if her sister's life were nothing more than a footnote in his twisted story.

Rage built inside her, fueled by the nonchalant tone that dismissed Amaya as if she were insignificant when, to Yaneriz, she was everything. Without thinking, she struck him on the back of the head with the gun. She was tired—tired of him, tired of Thompson, the park ranger, and every other person who had played a part in this nightmare. She wanted her sister back, and she was done with the games.

All you two have is each other. La Doña's words echoed in Yaneriz's mind, just as they had years ago when she and Amaya left for the U.S. after their father finally got them papers on their twelfth birthday. La Doña, unable to trust her son to raise the girls she now saw as her own, had convinced him to get her papers as well. He did. Soon, their already cramped apartment housed the three women who had become a family: La Doña, Yaneriz, and Amaya.

But the comfort of family didn't last. When they were sixteen, their father died, leaving them with debt instead of the security they had hoped for. La Doña tried to hold everything together, but cancer took its toll. She held on for as long as she could, until Yaneriz and Amaya turned nineteen.

By then, Amaya was in boot camp. Even as she lay dying, La Doña refused to let Amaya return. "I'm already dead," she had said. "You both are still living, so live and don't stop your life for the dead."

So it had been Yaneriz, not Amaya, holding her grandmother's hand, watching the life fade from her eyes. *All you two have is each other* were her final words—a blessing, a prayer, or maybe even a curse.

Yaneriz's vision blurred as guilt overwhelmed her. *I couldn't even do that. It should've been me.* The thought seared her brain. After losing their dad, then their grandmother—it should've been her. Not Amaya. Not the kind, patient, forgiving one. It should've been her.

"She's my sister. My only family," she muttered, her voice fractured.

Their uncles had been right, she thought bitterly. Yaneriz had been a burden to everyone. Not being able to accept her responsibilities had stressed their grandmother to death, and now it showed as she had been unable to protect her sister.

Defeated, Yaneriz followed Roberts, her heart heavy with shame.

But then, a familiar calm washed over her, the same comforting presence that had soothed her in the trunk of the car. *Abuela is here.*

"I'm sorry," she whispered, knowing the spirit of La Doña was near. The rest of her apology was silent, but she knew her grandmother could hear every word. *I'm sorry for all the things*

I put you through. I'm sorry for not protecting Amaya. I'm sorry for failing you both.

A tear rolled down her cheek, and in that moment of distraction, Roberts spun around and grabbed the gun from her. Yaneriz held on tight, but he punched her arm, making the gun fall from her grip.

Roberts took off, sprinting away from her.

"Fuck!" she groaned through clenched teeth, forcing herself to stoop, scooping up dirt and steel with a throbbing arm. She unlocked the safety, aimed, and shot. The shot cracked through the air, and Roberts crumpled to the ground.

Yaneriz waited, her breath shallow. Her shoulders collapsed when he didn't move. Tears burned the back of her eyes, but the violence, fear, and hatred that had filled her over the last twelve hours had hardened them. She wiped her nose against her shoulder, then approached cautiously.

Her chest tightened with rage. She didn't want Roberts to die so quickly. He didn't deserve the easy way out. Yaneriz stared at her hand holding the gun, the same hands that had once braided Amaya's hair.

All her life, she had thought she understood what the truth was—that good people fought, and bad people lost, that families protected one another no matter the cost. But that belief had been shattered long ago. Now, here she was, holding a gun, the truth of what she'd become weighing heavier than the weapon in her hand.

—La verdad y la realidad son dos cosas muy diferentes,—her grandmother's voice echoed in her memory. *Truth and reality are two different things.*

Was this reality? Was this the truth of who she had always been? Or was she simply a product of the nightmare life had thrown her into?

"Sorry, piece of shit," she whispered, standing over him. There was a part of her that wanted to kick him, to inflict the same indignities he had put her through and those she could only imagine he inflicted on her sister. But if she did, what would she become? Would she become just like him? Like Thompson? Instead, she kneeled by his legs, her hands shaking as she patted down his pockets. In the last pocket, she found it—a second phone.

"Hmm." She knew it held answers, but wasn't sure she was ready for them. With trembling hands, she held the phone to Roberts' face, unlocking it. Her stomach knotted as she scanned the messages.

The texts were damning, messages from an unknown number discussing her sister in the past tense, even mentioning Yaneriz. They had known about her. Yaneriz's breath came faster, her mind reeling. The text she had at first thought was Amaya, had been Roberts. He had texted it that, thinking Amaya used the same white-girl lexicon. Even the made up text conversation he showed her at Santo's Coffee Shop had been his doing.

Her fingers lost feeling. The phone fell from her hand, bouncing off Roberts' chest and hitting the ground with a hollow thud.

—Está bien, mi niña. Ve encuentra a tu hermana,— La Doña's voice urged.

But she picked up the phone to search for more. She needed to know where he hid her sister, and she didn't wonder long. Yaneriz found the answer to that question in his second phone. Her stomach churned as she read about the "burial of a pet." Vomit rose in her throat. They buried her like she was nothing; worse than an animal.

Yaneriz's hands shook violently as she followed the phone's flashlight, waving it back and forth across the ground. Her eyes landed on a patch of fresh dirt where the owl had hooted earlier. Her entire body went numb.

Dropping to her knees, she dug with her bare hands, clawing at the dirt. Her fingers were bleeding, nails broken, but she didn't stop. Desperation fueled her, and finally, her hand touched something solid.

The air left her lungs when her fingers grazed cold, hardened flesh. Gently, she cleared the dirt away until she saw it—Amaya's face. Decayed, distorted by whatever horrors she had endured, but unmistakably hers.

A sob broke free from Yaneriz, and she collapsed against her sister's grave, her entire body trembling. Tears poured from her eyes, mixing with the dirt and blood on her hands as she rocked back and forth, cradling herself in sorrow.

—Lo hiciste, mi niña. Encontraste a tu hermanita. Ahora ella puede descansar,— La Doña's voice said softly.

But Yaneriz couldn't find peace. Her cries filled the empty night.

"Why didn't you help her? Why didn't you tell me?" Her voice broke, hoarse from grief and fury.

—Los muertos no pueden hacer mucho. Ya estamos muertos,— her grandmother replied gently. —Tú tampoco puedes hacer mucho. El destino y las decisiones son de cada uno.—

"No!" Yaneriz screamed into the starless sky. If I'd known. If I'd checked sooner. If I hadn't been so willfully stubborn to refuse to see what all was there along; the signs at every post. Every 'what-if' echoed in her mind, tearing at her sanity.

—No te culpes,— La Doña whispered.

Yaneriz opened her mouth, but instead of words, another scream erupted from her, a raw cry filled with all her pain. She screamed at the night, at the spirits who had stayed silent, at the universe that let good people suffer.

When the last of her strength left her, Yaneriz collapsed into herself, hugging her knees. Her tear-filled eyes trailed Amaya's body seeing the wound that had called Yaneriz's heart, the wound that had probably killed her sister. She pressed her hand against her mouth keeping a scream from coming. Her eyes trailed to her sister's hand. It was then she noticed the blood under her sister's nails and something sticking out from her grasp.

Despite everything in her body screaming not to, she leaned forward and pulled the paper free. It was a sonogram.

Yaneriz's breath caught in her throat. The world tilted beneath her as the truth crashed down. Her sister had been pregnant. The air of mystery that surrounded every interaction had been this. She cradled the sonogram, her body trembling uncontrollably.

"Why?" she whispered, her voice shredded.

—Algunas veces el destino es corto, pero poderoso,— La Doña said.

Yaneriz shook her head at the absurdity. There was nothing powerful about Amaya's brief life. Her sister hadn't gotten the chance to live, and her baby never had the chance to be born.

She cupped her face in her hands, feeling the pulse of her throbbing temples. Nothing about this was right. Nothing could make it right.

TWO HOURS LATER, Yaneriz gathered the phones from
the men who killed her twin. She couldn't bring herself to
turn Thompson over and unlock his phone. Not out of guilt
for what she'd done to him, but because looking at him was
like staring into the heart of what had shattered her life. There
was only so much she could take. Instead, she focused on
Roberts' phones, unlocking both and taking screenshots of
everything. She created a new email account and sent the files
to herself.

Her grandmother's whispers in her ear reminded her of
everything she needed to hide or scrub clean. For that,
Yaneriz had been grateful. She retraced her steps, erasing any
proof she had been there. She knew it would only buy her
time—soon enough, a team of cops would scour the grounds,
find her phone, and pin the blame on her.

She knew how it worked for people like her—Black and
brown folks were guilty until proven innocent. And these
deaths weren't purely in self-defense. No. Untethered rage,
vengeance for the men who had murdered Amaya and tried
to get away with it fueled them.

The thought of the texts and emails she had uncovered

from Roberts' phones rekindled her anger. But she couldn't kill them twice. Her only hope was that scrubbing her presence from the scene would give her enough time to settle her affairs, be there when they brought Amaya's body back, and disappear before the cops came looking for her.

Yaneriz was certain the unsaved number on Roberts' burner phone belonged to Thompson. It all made sense now. Thompson wasn't supposed to be with Amaya, but he was. And when she told him she was pregnant and planned to keep the baby, he'd started plotting her death. They knew about Yaneriz—Amaya had likely mentioned her. But what they hadn't anticipated was that Yaneriz would show up unannounced. That threw a wrench into their plan, forcing them to rush and come up with a new one.

Suddenly, Yaneriz became the perfect scapegoat. Roberts, the mastermind, had covered his tracks by getting her fingerprints on the document she'd touched earlier, intending to use that to frame the story of rival sisters. Although rare, rival sisters crimes existed and a narrative where the antagonist was an *other*; a foreign person became too believable. It fit into the savage stereotype that was often put on people with her background. They had it all mapped out, carefully orchestrating a narrative where neither Thompson nor Roberts would be held accountable for what they'd done to Amaya.

As she turned the car around, ready to leave the campgrounds, she remembered the text she had received.

Don't trust Roberts.

Someone had tried to warn her.

A sudden thud from the back startled her. Slamming the brakes, the rental car jerked to a stop. Panic crept in—was someone lurking in the backseat? Her heart pounded as she unbuckled her seatbelt, unlocked the door, and gripped the car key between her fingers like a weapon.

The light from the open door illuminated the interior. At first, she saw nothing. Then, leaning in, she spotted her camera bag behind the passenger seat. Frantically, she dug through it and let out a sigh of relief when she found her phone. Roberts had turned it off to cover his tracks. Now it would hide hers. A small, bittersweet smile flickered across her face as she pulled back onto the road, following the exit sign out of the campgrounds.

Once on the highway, a strange sense of peace settled over her. It didn't belong to her—she knew that. She turned to the empty seat beside her. "¿Y Amaya?"

—Encontré a alguien caminando cerca que la va encontrar. Tú te tienes que ir de aqui—La Doña explained.

Leaving her sister's body behind, even near the men who had hurt her, felt impossible. But La Doña was right—she had to go. There was still so much to do.

Minutes passed in silence until La Doña spoke again, — Ella quiere estar contigo.—

A knot formed in Yaneriz's throat, choking back every word she wanted to say. She could only nod as grief trapped her voice.

Back in Killeen, Yaneriz entered Amaya's apartment, and the weight of loss hit her like a suffocating blanket. Grief wrapped around her, squeezing tighter with each breath. The sight of the wilted flowers made her knees buckle under the weight of it all. She pulled herself up and dragged herself to the bathroom, splashing cold water on her face, trying to ground herself.

Yaneriz forced herself to clean the apartment, putting everything back exactly as she'd found it. She knew now that it was Roberts who had left it in this state. The thought of his hands on Amaya's things made her tremble with disgust.

Each movement brought back flashes of the horror she had just lived, threatening to pull her back into the darkness. But she wrenched her focus away, fighting with every fiber of her being to stay present. "You can't focus on that, Yani. Not now," she whispered to herself.

The urge to curl up in her sister's bed and let grief swallow her whole was almost overwhelming—it would have been so easy to give in. But she couldn't. "You have to finish this," she told herself, forcing her trembling hands to keep moving.

After scrubbing the apartment of any trace of her presence, Yaneriz booked a redeye flight back to El Paso. She grabbed her things, changed into clean clothes from her sister's closet, and headed back to her rental. There was one more loose end to tie up.

———

Yaneriz opened the glove compartment and stared at the Fort Hood base pass. She had, in fact needed those three days. A tear trailed down her cheek at the thought. She drove back to her sister's job and parked outside the building. It was earlier than when she'd last been there, and she hoped to catch Williams before she went inside. Even though the windows were shut, a breeze moved through the car, and she knew her grandmother was with her.

—You can trust her,—La Doña whispered.

Yaneriz let out a relieved sigh. "How come I can hear you and feel you more now?"

Before, La Doña's presence had been fleeting, unexpected. Now, it was as though Yaneriz sensed her before she even spoke.

—Tu corazón ya está abierto a la posibilidad,—La Doña replied.

Yaneriz didn't fully understand, but as she reflected on it, she realized her grandmother was right. She hadn't been open to spirits or ghosts before. If it was something unseen, she hadn't put any relevance to it. She nodded, feeling La Doña's approving smile.

A question lingered on her lips. "You're not going to stay with Amaya?"

The mention of her sister made her throat swell with grief. She was still angry with La Doña, but the thought of facing this alone terrified her.

—Nunca voy a dejar a mis niñas. Voy a estar con las dos, —La Doña reassured her.

Yaneriz wanted to ask more. She wanted to speak with Amaya, to hear her voice again, to get her forgiveness. But guilt tightened in her chest like a vice—she wasn't ready to hear how badly she'd failed. Even though Amaya had once forgiven her after that childhood accident, when they both apologized, Yaneriz couldn't forgive herself. *And what if Amaya couldn't either?* The thought of it terrified her.

For now, having La Doña at her side, even in the form of a ghostly whisper, was enough. It had to be.

A few minutes passed before she spotted Williams in the parking lot. When Williams caught sight of her, she jogged over, slightly out of breath.

"Why the hell didn't you listen to me?" Williams asked, eyes wide with exasperation.

Yaneriz furrowed her brow in confusion.

"The text," Williams clarified, watching her carefully. "I know you read it."

It dawned on Yaneriz. The message from the unknown number... it had been Williams. She quickly pulled out her phone, showing her the warning.

Williams nodded and shook her head like she was scolding a child. "Yeah, that text. Damn, girl. Save my number. You'll probably need it again."

Yaneriz did as she was told without protest. Deep down, she knew that once this conversation was over, her mind might shut down. She might try to forget everything—like it had done after every trauma she had endured. Her brain would push it all away, only letting fragments surface during sleepless nights.

Once finished, she glanced up to find Williams studying her face, a flicker of something raw in her eyes.

"You look just like her," Williams said, voice softening.

The weight of that comparison hit Yaneriz like a fresh wave of grief. She lowered her head, the familiar sting of sorrow climbing from her chest to her throat. She was no longer one of two. There would be no more twin sister remarks. No more comparisons. No more Amaya.

Tears welled up before she could stop them.

"Damn... I'm sorry. That was out of line. I know better." Williams shifted awkwardly, clearly realizing the impact of her words.

"It's okay," Yaneriz whispered, wiping her nose with her sleeve. "I do look just like her." She took a shaky breath, pushing the grief down, trying to keep it from choking her entirely. "I... I need your help, Williams. If you don't mind."

Williams' face tightened, but her tone softened. "I didn't see you."

Yaneriz shook her head quickly. "No, no. The opposite. I was here. You saw me. I came in, looking for my sister. Roberts, your commander, and sergeant major—none of them helped me. Roberts tried to say something at Santo's Cafe but clammed up. They knew. They all knew, and I've been waiting for answers at my sister's place, but I didn't get any and now I have to go back to work."

Williams nodded slowly, taking it all in. "She was one of the good ones, you know? Kind, but not a pushover. Took care of her soldiers, even when it got her into trouble."

Hearing about this side of Amaya—a leader, a protector— struck Yaneriz in a way she hadn't expected. She blinked back more tears, biting her lip.

"I'm not surprised this happened to her, though," Williams

added, bitterness creeping into her voice. "They always get the good ones. When LTC Thompson took over, I was scared for her. There were rumors... There's always rumors. You know how it is—every unit has its dirty laundry, and we all hear about it. Amaya just didn't hang around the 'right' people, the ones who know things, who keep their ear to the ground. You know? She just kept to herself. Not a loner, just private."

Yaneriz nodded, trying to process it all, to imagine this other side of her sister. The SSG Alvarez that she'd barely known.

Williams kept going, her voice tight. "But when the rumors come from the top? Those are the hardest ones to pin down. Too many people work overtime to keep those quiet. I can't blame her for not knowing... Blaming her would make me just like them—the ones who always blame the victim."

Yaneriz felt her throat swell again.

Williams kept going. "She could've gone to the top," she said softly. "She could've been the one to change it."

A deep sadness settled over both of them. Yaneriz could see it clearly on Williams' face—a raw, unspoken grief. She wanted to ask more, to learn everything about Amaya's life as a soldier, to uncover all the details she'd missed. But fear held her back. What other horrors might surface? About her, about others. Perhaps about Williams herself. She didn't think she could bear it.

Instead, she pulled out her phone, hoping to change the trajectory of the conversation. "Let me show you what I found."

Yaneriz showed Williams everything she had pulled from Roberts' phones, even the files she'd managed to extract from Thompson's. Williams shook her head, her jaw tightening. "This shit... it's not gonna end."

"Can you do something with it?" Yaneriz asked hesitantly. "I mean... I thought maybe—"

Williams understood immediately. She took the phone from Yaneriz. "I know just the people to leak it to."

"WTF?" Yaneriz asked, thinking of the notorious social media pages that exposed Army scandals.

"No, not directly like that," Williams said, a small smirk on her lips. "I know someone who can get it to them, though."

Yaneriz nodded, relief washing over her as she watched Williams finish sending herself the files. La Doña had been right about Williams.

"Good luck," Williams called after her as Yaneriz turned back to her rental car.

———

Forty-five days later.

Yaneriz had known this moment would come. She'd tried to prepare herself. She'd practiced the breaths, the straightening of her spine, the setting of her jaw. She thought she could be ready. But as soon as she looked through the peephole, her heart lurched painfully, her legs buckling beneath her.

Her breath quickened, and she stepped back, swallowing hard.

No.

She couldn't pretend anymore. They were here.

She forced herself to look again, and there they were—two figures in uniform standing solemnly outside her door. A woman, clutching papers to her chest, her lips tight with restraint. And beside her, a man wearing a black beret with a cross, his presence like the final nail in the coffin.

Tears pricked her eyes.

"I can do this," Yaneriz whispered, her voice trembling, barely holding on to the lie.

With a shaking hand, she turned the knob and pulled the door open.

The air between them felt thick with the unspoken. The woman's expression wavered, as if the weight of the task was too heavy for her to bear. "Ma'am… are you Yaneriz Alvarez, the sister of Staff Sergeant Amaya Alvarez?" Her voice cracked.

Hearing her sister's name spoken aloud by strangers, spoken in the past tense, shattered whatever fragile barrier had held Yaneriz's grief at bay. Her chest tightened. The words she had thought she'd prepared shattered in her tongue like glass.

The man next to her, solemn and silent, watched with a gaze full of sorrow the small silver cross on his headgear, a symbol of finality she wasn't ready to face.

The tears that had been pooling in her eyes overflowed, streaming down her cheeks in uncontrollable waves. She didn't need to hear more. She already knew.

"I am," Yaneriz whispered, her voice collapsing under the crushing weight of those two words. The words that confirmed that Amaya was truly gone, and she was all that was left.

CHAPTER
SIXTEEN

AT AN UNDISCLOSED DINER, Yaneriz sat quietly, her stiff left arm aching more than usual. She forced a smile at the server who refilled her water and then brought her good arm up to cradle a still-hot double shot of espresso. The strong, bitter taste did nothing to soothe the heaviness in her chest as she watched the news flash on the TV above the counter. Every network was repeating the same story.

"Breaking News" flashed across the top and bottom of the screen in bold red, followed by the somber voice of the newscaster, a woman with straight brown hair and too-red lipstick. Yaneriz could barely focus on the words, but they cut through the diner's usual hum of clinking glasses and conversation.

"Devastating news from Fort Hood, Texas, a town already marred by scandal. Now, another tragic story. Staff Sergeant Amaya Alvarez, a Dominican American soldier who immigrated to the United States and joined the Army for a better life, is dead. But this death was not in defense of the Nation, Sean."

Yaneriz's grip tightened around the tiny cup, her knuckles whitening. The woman on the screen turned to her co-anchor before looking back at the camera. "Many are asking when this will finally stop."

The camera shifted to Sean, who gave a measured nod. "Are there any leads, Laura?"

Laura turned her head, caught between the co-anchor and the viewers at home. "An unidentified source has come forward with information. However, the police and Fort Hood both refuse to confirm any details, as their investigations remain ongoing."

The screen returned to Sean. "We'll keep our finger on the pulse of this story and provide updates as they come." With an unbothered smile, he transitioned to the next story, something about ducks reuniting with their mother. Yaneriz's heart clenched as the world continued, indifferent to the violence and death.

Her phone buzzed in her jacket pocket, pulling her back from the swell of rage bubbling inside her. She reached for it, careful not to disturb the backpack sitting on the seat next to her—the one with the urn that held Amaya's ashes.

Rolling her left shoulder to ease the stiffness, Yaneriz unlocked her phone. An email had come through from a forged address. She stared at the screen, feeling a sense of foreboding as she ran her hand over the back of her neck, the freshly shaved undercut pricking her fingers. For a moment, she debated whether to open it, the weight of the past few months making her hesitate. But then a familiar voice whispered in her ear.

—Abrelo.—

It was La Doña's voice. She promised she would stay and she had done just that.

With a deep breath, Yaneriz opened the email, her pulse quickening as she read the few chilling words:

I hope this is you. She was not the only one.

Yaneriz felt the familiar tightness return to her chest as she read the words again. Her hand quivered as she closed the email. The nightmare wasn't over. Amaya wasn't the only one. Someone else was out there, and they needed closure as she had needed it once.

ABOUT THE AUTHOR

Johanny Ortega (Joa) is a passionate storyteller, independent author, and publisher. She explores a wide range of genres, from middle-grade fiction to adult thrillers, horror, and fantasy. Writing under her given name, she captures the heartfelt and challenging experiences of children and families, while her pen name, **J.E. Ortega**, delves into the darker side of human nature.

Joa's stories are deeply personal, rooted in her own lived experiences and those of her Dominican heritage. Her characters speak in Spanglish, confront social issues, and often navigate immigrant experiences, creating a rich mosaic of diverse voices.

A fierce advocate for representation in literature, Joa's work spans not only fiction but also includes podcasting, blogging, and reviewing inclusive books that feature marginalized voices. On her podcast, *Have a Cup of Johanny*, she shares lessons learned, social commentary, and personal reflections, giving her audience a raw, vulnerable look into her world.

As a writer, she's on a mission to spotlight OWN voice stories, champion diverse reads, and offer readers emotional, thought-provoking narratives that stay with them long after the last page. When she's not writing, Joa spends her time in uniform, fights to spend more time with her husband, human and fur babies, and resting because this soft girl era is not going to start itself. To find out what she's writing next, head over to her website: haveacupofjohanny.com or find her on TikTok @acupofjo_hanny or on Threads.